'S... ...ed
up...

Incredulously, she ... ...ly why. You paid me ... ...!' she accused.

He raised his eyebrows. 'That's the first time someone's ever complained that I've *over*paid them,' he drawled.

'Don't be obtuse, Nikolai—you know exactly what I mean.'

'No, I don't. I thought you were good at your job and deserved the extra payment.'

'What? Or the *extra services* provided?'

He froze. 'You think that I'm the kind of man who *pays* for sex?'

'Can we keep your ego out of it for a moment? This isn't about *you*—it's about *me*,' she shot back, swallowing down the intense hurt she still felt at the memory of him waving that wretched envelope at her as if she was some kind of hooker. 'So why the over-generous gesture, if not for that?'

For a moment he was silent as he battled with his feelings, angry that she was forcing him to offer some kind of explanation—he who never had to explain himself to anyone. 'I realised that I'd misjudged you,' he said heavily. 'That you were not the woman I thought you to be.'

Sharon Kendrick started story-telling at the age of eleven and has never really stopped. She likes to write fast-paced, feel-good romances, with heroes who are so sexy they'll make your toes curl!

Born in west London, she now lives in the beautiful city of Winchester—where she can see the cathedral from her window (but only if she stands on tiptoe). She has two children, Celia and Patrick, and her passions include music, books, cooking and eating—and drifting off into wonderful daydreams while she works out new plots!

TOO PROUD
TO BE BOUGHT

BY
SHARON KENDRICK

MILLS
BOON

All the characters in this book have no existence outside the imagination of the author, and have no relation whatsoever to anyone bearing the same name or names. They are not even distantly inspired by any individual known or unknown to the author, and all the incidents are pure invention.

First published in Great Britain 2011
by Mills & Boon, an imprint of Harlequin (UK) Limited,
Eton House, 18-24 Paradise Road, Richmond, Surrey TW9 1SR

© Sharon Kendrick 2011

ISBN: 978 0 263 88652 8

Harlequin (UK) policy is to use papers that are natural, renewable and recyclable products and made from wood grown in sustainable forests. The logging and manufacturing process conform to the legal environmental regulations of the country of origin.

Printed and bound in Spain
by Blackprint CPI, Barcelona

TOO PROUD
TO BE BOUGHT

To David Small—a true knight in shining armour!

CHAPTER ONE

IT WAS like looking at a stranger.

A glamorous, sexy stranger.

Zara blinked in disbelief at the image which gleamed back at her from the long mirror—all curves and shadows and expanses of unaccustomed bare flesh. How long since she had looked like this—like a real woman instead of a drudge? Though come to think of it, she could never remember looking quite like *this* before.

The acid-green satin dress clung to her body like syrup, delicate fabric pooling to the floor in a silken stream. It was light years away from her usual jeans and sloppy T-shirts—but the differences didn't stop there. Her eyes looked huge and sooty above carefully highlighted cheekbones and her usual ponytail had been replaced with a slick and grown-up chignon, leaving her bare neck feeling curiously vulnerable. Fake diamonds sparkled at her throat and hung in glittering waterfalls from her ears. She narrowed her eyes. Didn't she look just a little…*ostentatious*?

Resisting the urge to chew on her carefully manicured nails, she looked down at her friend, who was kneeling on the floor at her feet. 'Emma, I can't,' she croaked.

'Can't what?' Emma gave the silken hem of the dress a final tug.

'I can't gatecrash this party—I'm a waitress, not a socialite! I can't target some mystery Russian billionaire because you think he'd be good for your business. And I can't carry off wearing the kind of outfit which makes me feel as if I'm not wearing anything at all. Shall I go on?'

Emma took the pin out of her mouth. 'Rubbish! Of course you can. You'll be doing us both a favour. *I* get to showcase one of my dresses to one of the world's richest men—and *you* get your first night out since heaven only knows when. Believe me, Zara, chances like this don't come along very often. Nikolai Komarov owns department stores in every major city in the world and he's a connoisseur of beautiful women. He's itching to have me design a collection for him or to clothe his latest mistress—he just doesn't know it yet!'

Zara glanced down at the gossip magazine which was open to reveal a black and white photo of the Russian oligarch and more doubts pricked over her skin as his pale and strangely intense eyes seemed to bore straight into her like twin laser beams. 'And I'm supposed to give him your business card?'

'Why not?'

'Because…because it's like I'm going to be touting for trade at a social occasion.'

'Nonsense. They'll all be doing it. It's what's known in the business world as networking. It isn't as if you're hurting anybody, is it? And anyway, *you* could do with something like this. How long is it since you had any real enjoyment?'

Enjoyment? Zara's fingers tightened around the little feathered concoction of a handbag she was holding because her friend's question had touched a nerve. And maybe the nerve was rawer than she'd thought. It *did* seem an eternity since she had been out anywhere—unless it was to the grocery store or pharmacy at the end of the road. Her beloved godmother's final illness had dragged on and on until death had seemed like a release from all the little indignities and sadnesses she had borne along the way.

For months, Zara's life had been dominated by the sickroom while she had nursed the woman who hadn't even been a blood relative. But her loyalty to the lady who'd taken her in after the death of her parents meant that she'd dropped her studies to care for her without a second thought. Day and night she had juggled meals, care, bills and medicines—and waitressing for Emma's mother's catering company whenever she could squeeze it in.

And when it had all been over, and the last of the all-too-few sympathy cards had been read, Zara had felt lonely and bereft. As if too much had happened for her to ever contemplate returning to the carefree student life she'd known before. There were still debts to be settled, too—and her grim determination not to lose the little house she'd been bequeathed seemed to dominate her thoughts. An unknown future lay ahead of her, and it was scary.

'So why not *have* a little fun, Zara? Why not be a Cinderella for the night and dance all your cares away? You know you'll be doing me a huge favour.'

Zara gave a wry smile as Emma's voice butted into her thoughts. Could she? If only cares could simply be danced away—how much simpler the world would be. Yet maybe her friend was right. What *was* stopping her from having a little light-hearted diversion? Unless she was secretly yearning for the alternative scenario of yet another night spent worrying about the stack of unpaid bills, which wouldn't seem to go away...

'Okay,' she said, drawing her shoulders back and taking one last look at her reflection. 'I'll go. I'll enjoy wearing this exquisite gown you've created and try to enjoy being on the other side of a tray for once—drinking the champagne instead of handing it out! And I'll walk up to this Russian oligarch of yours and give him your card. How's that?'

'Perfect! I've primed the other waitresses about it and they think it's a wonderful idea. I guess they can't really object, since my mum is the one who's employing them and she's not even in the country! Now go! Go on—go!'

Clutching the crumpled money her friend had thrust at her, Zara walked out of the small studio in too-high heels and hailed the welcoming light of a black cab before she had time to change her mind about a scheme which seemed to be growing crazier by the second.

The summer evening was still light and every flower in the capital seemed to be in bloom, but as the taxi drew up outside the Embassy her heart began to race. What if she was discovered—a humble waitress masquerading as a bonafide guest? An *imposter* who had no right to be there. Wouldn't they throw her out and kick up the most tremendous fuss in the process? Yet the man who collected her ticket at the door did nothing other than flick her a quick, admiring glance and Zara drew a deep breath as she walked into the gleaming ballroom.

The vast room looked spectacular. Glittering chandeliers threw diamond lights over tall vases of scarlet roses and a string quartet was playing on a raised dais in front of a shiny, bare dance-floor. She glanced at the other guests and thought how amazing they looked.

Especially the female guests. *Their* diamonds were the real thing and surely that stood out by a mile. Was the rich Russian really going to be impressed by what she was wearing—a hand-crafted gown made by an ambitious young fashion student—when there was so much screamingly expensive couture in this room?

She could see a couple of men turning round to glance at her and their women partners following suit. Could they guess that she was operating outside her comfort zone—that she was actually *trespassing*? Suddenly, Emma's mad scheme seemed destined to fail and, nervously, Zara grabbed a glass of champagne from a girl she'd worked with on countless occasions and took a mouthful of cold wine. The alcohol relaxed her a little—especially when a couple of the other waitresses she knew winked and murmured hello in passing.

But something was making her feel uncomfortable—some sixth sense, which told her she was being watched.

Now you're just being paranoid, she told herself.

Yet the sensation persisted as she moved through the glamorous throng until she found her eyes being drawn unwillingly to a man who was standing at the far end of the ballroom.

And suddenly, she couldn't stop looking.

It was like seeing a drop of blood on virgin snow—because he stood out from everyone else in the room. His hair was the colour of beaten gold, his eyes were glacially blue and he possessed a hard and arrogant mouth, which spoke of experience and sensuality. Zara realised that the man's high, sculpted cheekbones and piercing eyes were oddly familiar—and then she realised why. She felt a shiver whisper over her skin. It was Nikolai

Komarov—the Russian oligarch, and the man she was supposed to be targeting.

Her first thought was that his photo hadn't done him justice—on the page he had been appealing but in the flesh he was perfect. And her second thought was that he was the most intimidating man she had ever seen. His face made her think of a diamond—with its hard, sculpted angles and those cold, glittering eyes. And as for the rest of him...

Zara swallowed down an unfamiliar kind of hunger. Powerful, wealthy tycoon he might be, but, more than anything, he was pure and unbridled masculinity.

A beautifully cut suit moulded his body, emphasising wide shoulders, solid torso and narrow hips, which tapered down to long, muscular legs. He held himself tall and very straight, and stood so still that for a moment Zara thought he might almost have been made from wax, rather than from flesh and blood. But waxen eyes did not gleam like that, did they? And nor did they focus with unmoving scrutiny on their subject—the way he was doing with her. It felt like having all the breath punched from her body as she found herself captured in his cold yet searing gaze.

From his position at the far end of the room, Nikolai saw the woman glance over at him and felt his body tense, although a woman looking at him was nothing new. Women looked at him all the time. Though not usually like that, he conceded. Like a startled little deer who'd just spied the big, bad hunter deep in the forest...

Who the hell *was* she? He'd noticed her the moment she'd walked into the ballroom in that clinging green gown and he had been watching her ever since. His expression grew thoughtful. Something about her made her stand out from the crowd of overdressed women and he couldn't work out what it was. How come she'd ignored everybody in the room except to smile rather nervously at the waitresses?

With the practised look of the connoisseur, his eyes swept over her in lazy assessment. Unlike most of the women here tonight, her face wasn't stiffened with Botox and her hair had the natural shine of youth. But it was her body which was the real showstopper. He felt a sudden flare of lust as he acknowledged that her body was absolutely *amazing*. All curves and seductive hollows and none of the gaunt look of the over-dieted. He let his gaze drift downwards over her bare shoulders—at skin which gleamed as softly as silk—to where her pert and luscious breasts formed a cleavage which was like an open invitation to a man's lips.

He put down his barely touched glass of champagne onto a passing waitress's tray. Nikolai's interest was piqued. He quirked her a smile he only ever used sparingly, and waited for the inevitable. Any minute now and she would start walking towards him with a hopeful little look of expectation on her face.

She didn't.

Nikolai's eyes narrowed as the woman seemed to hesitate, before turning away and beginning to walk in the opposite direction. And for a moment he couldn't quite believe it.

She had turned her back on him!

Now his interest was definitely alerted. All the hunter instincts which usually lay dormant—made redundant by modern women who preferred to do the chasing—rose to heat his blood. Was she playing games? Had she turned away simply to give him the opportunity to feast his eyes on the delectable swell of her buttocks? Nikolai's gaze was drawn irresistibly to the twin satin-covered globes and he swallowed. Because nobody could deny that it was a very delectable bottom indeed...

Like a puppet who was having his strings twitched by some unseen fingers, he began to tail her.

Zara could feel the little hairs on the back of her neck prickling and the sudden race of her heart as she moved through the ballroom. She wasn't being paranoid and she wasn't imagining it. He *was* following her! The intimidatingly handsome Russian with the icy stare who had been standing as still as a waxwork was now pursuing her across the room with a sure stealth.

She swallowed. Had he rumbled her? Guessed that she was an imposter with no earthly right to be here? In which case, wouldn't it just be best if she headed for the door, grabbed a bus and then phoned Emma with the news that her idea had been a disaster and that they should never have entertained it for more than a second? Because suddenly, the idea of waltzing up to him and presenting him with a business card seemed the height of crassness. What had given her the idea that she would have the nerve to do something like *that*?

Risking a quick glance over her shoulder, she could see that he had been swallowed up by the crowd and she speeded up as much as her impractical shoes would allow. Shielded by a cluster of guests, she ducked behind a huge marble pillar and stayed there for long enough to convince herself that she'd shaken him off. And when she came out, there was no sign of him. That rather daunting presence and those piercing eyes were nowhere to be seen. Quashing down an unmistakeable pang of disappointment, she glanced around, realising that she could make her escape, and...

'Hey.'

Zara froze as a deep accent she'd never heard cut through the jumble of her thoughts, some bone-deep instinct telling her that it was him. It could *only* be him. And reflecting how unfair life could be—that a man who looked like some sort of golden and dangerous god should have the kind of voice which sent tingles down a woman's spine just by uttering a word which managed to sound like both a command and a question. *Ignore him*, she told herself. *Pretend you haven't heard him and carry on walking.*

She made to take a step forward but he spoke again and she found her feet frozen into immobility by his silken question.

'Are you trying to run away from me?'

Short of being rude and causing a scene, Zara knew that she had no choice other than to brazen it out. Pinning what she hoped was a confident smile to her lips, she turned to face him, her heart hammering beneath the thin silk of her dress. 'Why, do you think I *should* run away from you?' she questioned calmly.

'Well, that rather depends,' he murmured as his eyes drifted over her body.

Yet even as Zara felt her skin tingle in response to his unashamed appraisal she knew that this was dangerous. Very dangerous. He was flirting with her—and in a way which was completely outside her comfort zone. Yet what could she do other than to play the part of the sophisticate she had been dressed to look like—even if inside she suddenly felt like a scared little girl who was out of her depth? She tried to remember the kind of things which seasoned flirts said on television programmes.

'Really?' She widened her eyes. 'On what?'

Nikolai's lips gave a flickering curve of satisfaction. This was better. Much better. For a moment back then, he had thought she meant it—that she was actually giving him the brush-off. And when had that last happened? Never, he reflected sagely. He might have been described as the world's biggest commitment-phobe, but he was a master at getting women into his arms. He felt the quick beat of pleasure as he realised that up close she was just as delicious. 'On whether you're any good at dealing with difficult and demanding men,' he mused.

It was such an outrageous thing to say that for a moment Zara forgot that all she was supposed to be doing was showcasing her friend's dress. She found herself remembering all the fantastic people in the caring professions she'd met when she'd been nursing her godmother and all the difficult conditions they had to endure every day. And then she compared their stoicism with the arrogance she saw written on this man's handsome face.

She found herself studying his costly black dinner suit—the price of which could probably have fed a family of four for at least a month. She thought about the pile of medical bills she'd been left with, and some rogue streak of rebellion made itself known. And besides, wasn't it better to concentrate on indignation rather than acknowledge the dizzying effect he was having on her senses?

'Most people don't confess to their faults on a first meeting,' she commented drily.

Icy blue eyes glittered with mischief. 'Aren't you rather taking it for granted that there's going to *be* a second meeting?' he questioned softly. 'And isn't that a little presumptuous of you, or is that what you've grown to expect from men—their instant capitulation and desire to see you again?'

Her experience of men was so small that Zara wanted to laugh—and the idea that someone like her should have men *capitulating* was even funnier. Especially a man as gorgeous as this one, who was clearly living in a parallel universe. 'Actually, I never take anything for granted,' she answered. 'And I certainly try to avoid generalisations about the opposite sex.'

Nikolai's eyes narrowed as he heard a note in her voice which he couldn't quite define. Something which sounded a little like...*censure*? Once again, he felt a stir of interest. 'You know, I get the distinct sense that you don't approve,' he observed softly.

Now Zara sensed an even greater danger. Instinct told her to move away and yet another instinct—one which was much more powerful—kept her rooted to the spot. She stared up into the icy glitter of his blue eyes and her heart missed a beat. 'Of what?'

'Of me, *milaya moya*. Of me.'

'How can I possibly have an opinion about you, when we're complete strangers?' she questioned.

'Yes, we are,' he agreed. 'But that is something which is easily remedied.' He gave a brief smile as he watched closely to see whether his name might stir any sign of recognition. 'My name is Nikolai Komarov.'

Zara felt her throat thicken, knowing that now was the time to look at him and to say, very calmly: *Actually, I already knew that. I also know that you are a hugely influential man with your own department stores as well as innumerable gorgeous girlfriends—and my friend happens to be a very talented designer. Do you like the dress I'm wearing? Actually, it's one of hers. Perhaps I could give you one of her cards and you might think about looking at her collection?* But as those palely intense eyes studied her she knew that she couldn't go through with it. She couldn't. Was that because she was enjoying the fantasy of flirting with him? Of pretending she really *was* the person she was dressed up to be instead of some broke little waitress who was doing a friend a favour? 'You're…you're Russian,' she said slowly.

'How very perceptive of you.' But Nikolai felt his mouth tighten with an odd kind of disappointment. So it had *not* been an instant eyes-across-a-room thing after all. She *had* heard of him—he would have staked his fortune on that. He had seen the signs of suppressed recognition too many times in the past and he had seen it flare in her eyes. But he didn't know why he should be either surprised or disappointed—because women always played these games, didn't they? They lied. They indulged in subterfuge. They would open their pretty eyes very wide and insist that black was white—and sometimes he suspected they even ended up believing it themselves. 'You know many Russians, perhaps?'

'No. None at all.'

'Until now, of course.'

'Until now,' she agreed, with a slightly nervous smile. Would he be appalled if he knew who she was—an imposter who had no right to be here? She searched for clues in his face. Good guy or bad guy? Or just a wickedly hot guy who was used to getting whatever he wanted from a woman?

'And you are?' he prompted.

His icy eyes were cutting through her defences as he waited for her to respond and for a moment Zara was half tempted to give him a false name. A bogus identity to go with her one-off appearance—until she told herself how stupid that was. She would never see him again after tonight. A name like hers meant nothing to a man like this.

'I'm…Zara,' she said falteringly. 'Zara Evans.'

'A beautiful name,' he mused softly, observing that cute tremble of her lips. 'To go with a very beautiful woman.'

The throwaway compliment made her skin glow—it seemed like for ever since someone had paid her one, and nobody had ever called her beautiful before. But Zara told herself that she mustn't fall for his charm. He probably came out with statements like that every minute of every day—slick, perfectly timed statements, which were guaranteed to have women falling under his spell. She opened her mouth to say something smart and instead it came out as a breathless little 'th-thank you' and she could have kicked herself.

'Can I get you a drink, Zara?'

She shook her head. 'No, thanks—I've already had one.'

'Oh, I think you're allowed more than one.' He stared straight into her eyes. 'Though no more than two.' He smiled slightly to show he was teasing her.

He was making it sound as if the two of them were involved in some kind of conspiracy and the thought of *that* made Zara draw herself up short. What the hell did she think she was doing? This wasn't why she was supposed to be here—and if she had lost her nerve about foisting one of Emma's cards on him, then she ought to make herself scarce.

Because this man was dangerous—hadn't he told her so himself? 'Actually, I'd better go.'

'Why?'

'Because…' Her words tailed away as she tried to think of a good reason why she might wish to leave a party when she had only just arrived.

'You don't really have a reason, do you?' he questioned as he saw her bite her lip in a moment of indecision, which was oddly appealing. 'Not when there is music playing and I'm being plagued by an urgent desire to dance with you, which simply won't go away. So come here.'

To Zara's horror, he reached out and laced her fingers with his and began to lead her through the throngs of people. Well, maybe horror wasn't the right word, she conceded as people began to part to let them through. Excitement might have been more accurate. She could feel hot colour flaring at her cheeks as she became aware of heads turning to watch them and the pulse at her wrist began to hammer wildly beneath his fingertips. But it wasn't until he had halted by the small space of floor directly in front of the musicians that she tipped her head up to gaze at him.

'We can't dance!' she whispered.

'Why not?'

'Because—'

'Stop saying "because". Come and dance with me instead.' His icy eyes glittered out a cool challenge. 'You know you want to.'

And the awful thing was that he was right. She did. There was a melting, yearning pool in the pit of her stomach, which was longing for him to pull her into his arms—and when he did she gave an instinctive intake of breath, which caused his fingers to tighten around her waist.

'You see?' he murmured. 'It's what you wanted all along.'

Zara felt dizzy. What could she do? His hands had moved down and were now lying on her hips, the fingers splayed against the silk of her dress with a lazy and proprietary ease so that for a moment it felt as if he were touching the bare flesh beneath.

'Relax,' he instructed softly.

'How can I relax when everybody is looking at us?'

'You should just ignore them—or get used to it. The men are looking at us because they envy me, and the women because they wish they were standing where you were standing, *milaya moya*.'

It was an arrogant assessment, though Zara doubted that the first part was true. Why would the men envy Nikolai? Especially when there were loads of women in the room who were more attractive than her—rich, titled women who would probably be dancing confidently instead of worrying that they were going to spear his foot with one of their lethal heels.

Yet the soft music was very seductive and more seductive still was the way in which he pulled her towards him—almost before she realised he'd done it. She could feel the jut of his hips against hers and suddenly she became aware of the formidable heat of his hard body pressing into hers and could sense the desire which radiated from his powerful frame. Zara swallowed.

'Relax. You seem rather uptight,' he commented as an irresistible tug of desire shot through him.

She felt the almost careless caress of his thumb at her waist. What could she say—that the last time she'd had a slow dance with a man had been at some awful, noisy club, and it had felt *nothing* like this?

'I'm not used to dancing,' she said.

'Why not?'

Her face inches away from his shoulder, Zara wondered how best to answer him. Even if she hadn't been tied to the sickroom for the past however many months, she still couldn't have imagined herself whirling around a formal ballroom like this. It seemed rather old-fashioned.

She risked a glance up at his hard-boned face. How

old was *he*? Difficult to say, but certainly a lot older than her. He had experience written on every sculpted angle and there were faint lines of cynicism etching the sides of his mouth. Yet there was nothing old-fashioned about the way he was holding her, or the way it was making her pulse rocket. It felt elemental. As if dancing were something far too intimate to be doing in front of a crowd of people… 'Because—'

'There you go. That wretched word again.' He pulled her closer and felt her soft flesh yielding to his as he bent his head to her long neck and, closing his eyes, he inhaled her subtle scent. Was it roses he could smell? 'Didn't anyone ever tell you that repetition is boring?'

'You asked me a question and I was answering it,' she protested.

'I know I did. But suddenly I'm much more interested in the language of your body.'

'That's *outrageous*!'

He bent his lips to her ear. 'I know it is. But you're making me feel outrageous. Don't you feel a little outrageous, too, Zara?'

'No.'

'Yes, you do,' he demurred softly. 'Go on. Be brave. Admit it.'

End the dance, she told herself fiercely as she began to feel even more out of her depth. *End it now. Walk out of the ballroom and don't stop until you've reached the street. If you do it firmly then he's not likely to risk a scene by trying to stop you.*

But it was difficult to do anything other than to let the sweet strains of the string instruments lull her and the power of his touch wash over her senses. Zara could feel the slide of silk over her skin as she moved in time to the music, and she could feel the barely touching sensation of his fingers pressing against her flesh. A shiver of longing rippled over her flesh, a sensation so unexpected and unwanted that she felt the sudden thunder of her heart. Did he feel it, too? Was that why he positioned himself so that they were fractionally closer and her body seemed to be silently screaming that it wanted to be closer still? She had to stop all this—she *had* to, before she made a complete and utter fool of herself.

She pulled away from him with the reluctance of someone who was being forced to leave a warm fire to face a freezing blizzard outside. 'I really must go,' she said.

He nodded, knowing that if he stayed on the dance-floor with this rapidly escalating sense of arousal, then soon any kind of movement might prove impossible. And yet her abrupt ending of the dance made him reluctant to let the evening end—and he wasn't quite sure why. Because he was the one who usually called all the shots, who made the decision when to leave and when to stay?

'Okay. I'll take you home.' He saw her lips open and he shook his head. 'And before you go through the motions of protesting, you must realise that I'm not going to allow you to go home on your own.' Especially not looking like that, he thought. Not with the tight buds of her nipples outlined with such erotic clarity against the gleam of the emerald silk. 'Unless you have your own car waiting outside?' he questioned unevenly.

Could she swing it? Zara wondered. Convince him that one of those purring black limos which were clogging the streets around the embassy actually belonged to her? And then what? She could imagine him insisting on seeing her to the car and then the shame of having to admit that she was nothing but a fraud. She shook her head. 'No, I came by taxi. Um, where do you live?' she hedged.

'I have a house on the other side of the park.'

In a moment of real indecision, she looked at him until she realised that she was about to throw away a heaven-sent opportunity. Why *not* take up his offer? Mightn't she get the chance to hand over Emma's business card before she said goodnight? He had already admired the way she looked, so maybe she could turn round and tell him it was all her friend's handiwork. 'Okay, then… thank you—I will. But as I live a little…farther out—the car can drop you off first, and then take me on to my place afterwards.'

Nikolai ran a thoughtful finger over his lips. He thought that sounded like a very abrupt conclusion to an evening he had no desire to see end. At least, not yet. With a sudden ache, he acknowledged the sharpening to his senses which this fresh-faced minx seemed to have provoked. He'd been working so hard lately. Tunnelling all his energy and vision into his latest ambitious project, which meant that sex had been sidelined. And his last mistress had drained him with her tiresome requests that he 'make an honest woman of her'. Was there an honest woman in the world? he wondered bitterly. If so, he had yet to meet her. He flicked Zara a look which was now speculative.

'Let's go,' he murmured.

CHAPTER TWO

A BLACK limousine was waiting as they emerged from the ambassador's residence into the fragrant warmth of the evening and Zara felt as if she were stepping into a different world. Smoothly, the chauffeur opened the door for her and she sank onto the back seat and started looking around with a sense of wonder. What a car! The interior looked and smelt of pure luxury, all subtle and intoxicating and soft cream leather. And when Nikolai slid his long-legged frame in beside her and turned his head to look at her she could feel the sudden thunder of her heart. In the dim, enclosed space his proximity seemed even more potent than it had done on the dance-floor and Zara found herself wondering about the wisdom of travelling home with such a devastatingly sexy stranger.

'You know, it's still very early,' he observed slowly, watching the tiny pulse which flickered so frantically at her temple.

Zara found that there was nowhere to look other than at the compelling gleam in his eyes. 'So it is,' she observed lightly.

He liked the way that her hair was a woven mass of caramel and sunshine and he wanted to remove all the clips and see it tumble down around her shoulders. He could see the outline of her legs through the silk of her dress—slender, lean legs—and he felt another sharp ache of desire. 'And we're very close to my house,' he said, as if the thought had only just occurred to him. 'You could always come in for a quick drink, if you wanted.'

Zara's thoughts were scrambled by the frantically conflicting messages firing between body and brain. A strange man inviting you into his house for a nightcap was a definite no-no. And yet this was not any man—this just happened to be the most devastatingly attractive man she'd ever met. Wasn't Cinderella allowed a little glimpse of the prince's palace before her clothes returned to rags?

'I *could*.'

'But you're not sure?'

'What do you think?'

'I think you want to.'

Zara gave an uncertain laugh. 'It isn't always wise just to do what you want.'

'No? I've always thought exactly the opposite. That life is much too short to be dictated to by social etiquette.' His eyes narrowed. 'What if I give you my word that we'll have one quick drink and then my car will take you wherever you want to go? How does that sound?'

It sounded like madness—complete and utter madness—and yet it also sounded like the most tantalising offer she had received in a long time. Zara's world had been coloured bleak and sombre by recent events—could anyone really blame her if she wanted to peek at a more vibrant version of how life could be lived? One where shiny limousines picked you up from fancy parties and silent drivers sat and took you wherever you wanted to go.

But something stopped her and maybe it was the

realisation that this was outside her realm of experience on so many levels. Instinct told her she was dealing with a seasoned and experienced man. He was like a lion, she thought suddenly, her eyes straying to his thick mane of hair—deep and lustrous as beaten-gold. And a woman should not go into a lion's lair unless she was expecting to be eaten...

She shook her head. 'It's very sweet of you,' she said, and drew a breath with the same kind of determination which had seen her successfully battle with the doctors to keep her godmother at home during the final days of her life. 'But I don't think it's such a good idea.'

He could see that she meant it and for a moment Nikolai was surprised. Usually, he had to fight women off and had taken her acceptance as a given—especially when invitations to his home were precious and few. Yet her refusal intrigued as well as surprised him.

'Are you sure?' he questioned.

'Quite sure,' she said, with more conviction than she felt.

'Well, in that case...'

There was a heartbeat of a pause as he leaned across the space and stared down into her widening eyes and soft lips. 'I'll just have to kiss you goodnight right here—won't I, *milaya moya*?'

Her fingers gripped the soft leather seat. 'And do you always kiss women you hardly know goodnight?' she asked breathlessly.

'Not always, *net*. But you have been tantalising me all night—ever since you started running away from me at the party. And I can't remember the last time I had to chase a woman, quite literally in your case.'

If only he knew *why* she had been running! Suddenly Zara felt stricken with guilt. 'But—'

'Shut up,' he said, almost gently as he bent his mouth to hers.

Afterwards, she blamed the champagne—and his experience—because she did nothing to stop him. But it was more than cold wine on an empty stomach. It was hunger and it was curiosity. It had been a long time since Zara had been kissed. And no man had ever kissed her the way Nikolai Komarov proceeded to do in the back seat of his chauffeur-driven limousine.

All it took was one careless graze of his mouth and she began to tremble in response, causing him to make a small sound of assertion underneath his breath as he pulled her closer. And perhaps it was the comfort of being held like that which made Zara want to melt against him. The warm human contact which made her feel normal again, instead of the person who had become invisible and isolated from the rest of the world by sickness. How long since she had been cuddled—or felt any kind of security? With a hungry little cry, she lifted her fingers and tangled them in the thick, beaten gold of his hair and lost herself in the sweetness of his kiss.

Nikolai gave an unsteady laugh as his hand slid across her back, the rawness of her response startling him a little. He had expected sophistication—an erotic routine which she had gone through many times before. And yet the helpless trembling of her body did not go with her smooth, sleek image. Not at all. And wasn't there more than a little *tenderness* about the way she held him? He swallowed as he drew his mouth away and smoothed a fallen strand of hair away from her cheek—because tenderness wasn't something he encountered very often and it was curiously persuasive.

'You have great passion, I think,' he murmured.

'Do I?' she breathed.

'*Da*. Beautiful passion.'

His mouth sought hers once more and it was then that the kiss began to change. Zara gasped as his lips suddenly became more seeking and she found her own opening beneath them. She could sense the tension in his body as his hands splayed over her back, where her flimsy evening dress was cut away to reveal a large keyhole in the material. She could feel his fingers kneading against her bare skin as time slowed and she felt as if she had entered an intimate little world. One where Nikolai's tongue inside the warm cavern of her mouth made her feel as if she were being dragged down into some dark and erotic vortex.

'Nikolai—'

'What?' he growled.

'This is—'

'Amazing,' he purred, briefly lifting his head so that his eyes glittered out their unashamed desire, before tracing his finger over the fleshy trembling of her bottom lip. '*Da. Da.* I know it is.'

She had been about to say that it was wrong—and yet her body was telling her otherwise. Could something be wrong when it felt so right? she pondered distractedly. When his fingers were now tiptoeing down her neck towards her breasts, before skating with practised ease to alight on the aching swell of one silk-covered nipple.

Zara swallowed down the dryness in her throat. 'This is cr-crazy,' she gasped as his mouth bent to one aching breast.

Nikolai flicked his tongue over the thin silk, which was the only barrier between him and her bare nipple, as he heard her whispered little gasp. Did it make her feel better if she let herself protest about what they were doing, he wondered cynically, even though she clearly wanted him just as much as he wanted her?

But women were contrary creatures—he knew that. Often they liked to disguise their own earthy desire for fear that a man was judging them for being too 'easy'. Should he reassure her now that he didn't give a curse about convention and that she could be as 'easy' as she liked.

He drifted his hand down over one slender hip, his mouth briefly leaving the now-moist material of her gown and noting that he had left a darkened ring over her breast. 'You do realise that you have the most fantastic body?' he questioned. 'And that your dress shows it off quite beautifully.'

She shook her head, only dimly aware that she was blowing the opportunity to talk about the dress. 'St-stop it,' she whispered.

'Stop complimenting you? I thought all women liked to be complimented.'

'That's not what I meant,' she breathed. 'I meant, that you shouldn't be doing…*that*.'

'But you like me doing *that*.' He felt her little squirm of acquiescence. 'And you don't want me to stop it, do you?'

'I…do.'

'No, you don't. You want me to move my hand down to your ankle, don't you? Like this.'

'Nikolai!' Zara swallowed as his index finger made a provocative little circling movement there.

'And then I think you want me slowly to slide it up underneath your dress. Like this, *da*?'

'Nikolai,' she breathed as she felt the brush of his hand resting on the curve of her calf.

'Why, you're not even wearing any stockings,' he

observed unevenly. 'Just bare legs. What a very wicked young lady you are. No wonder that dress was clinging so provocatively to you as you walked into the ballroom.'

'Oh!' She could feel the sudden spring of her body in response to his feather-light touch—as if it had been woken from a deep, deep sleep and all her senses had suddenly come to urgent life.

'Listen, we're really very close to my house,' he said unevenly as the car slid to a halt at some traffic lights. He was so aroused by their encounter that he could barely get the words out and only supreme self-control stopped him from continuing what they were doing. But he really couldn't make love to her in the middle of a busy London street, could he? Not with his chauffeur sitting behind the darkened screen and the possibility of some damned traffic warden rapping on the window. 'Why don't you change your mind and come up for a drink?'

Zara stilled. Perhaps it was the blatant falsehood about having a drink when they both knew what was *really* on his mind—and on hers—which made common sense crash into her mind like a dark spectre. That and the fact that she was making out in the back of a car with a man she barely knew—*and she was risking ruining her friend's precious dress along with her own reputation!*

Her heart thudding, she pushed his hand away and slithered to the far end of the seat, her trembling fingers groping for her feathered handbag, which lay beside her like a wounded bird. 'No!'

His eyes narrowed but he felt the unmistakeable flicker of irritation. 'Isn't it a little late in the day for game-playing?'

'I'm not playing…' But the words died on her lips because she *was*. She *was* playing games. Dangerous games.

Pretending to be something she wasn't. Masquerading as his wealthy equal. Maybe that kind of women did make easy love to men they'd just met at a party—but she wasn't one of them. She amended her choice of words to allow her to extricate herself with a modicum of dignity. 'I'm sorry, but it's very late—and I'm tired.'

Nikolai felt the sharp spear of disappointment. Saw from the look on her face that she meant it—and he bit back his frustration. Of *course* she was playing games, probably in the mistaken belief that her refusal would make him think more highly of her. His mouth hardened. Did he have the time or the inclination to go through the necessary number of dates which she decreed obligatory before she let him take her to bed? Was she, he asked himself brutally, worth it?

His eyes drank in the wide green eyes, the flushed cheeks and the kiss-bruised lips and he felt a pulse begin to flicker at his temple. Yes, she was worth it—for novelty value as well as her curiously fresh-faced appeal. Because when was the last time a woman had actually turned him down?

'Well, I think that's a pity,' he said softly, reaching for his jacket pocket. But before Nikolai could extract one of the business cards he kept there he saw that she was pushing open the car door and swinging her shapely legs out and his brows knitted together in disbelief.

'Where the hell do you think you're going?'

'Home.'

'I told you that my driver would take you wherever you wanted to go.'

Zara shook her head. 'And I've changed my mind. I don't want a lift, thank you.'

'You don't?' His eyes narrowed incredulously. 'Why not?'

Zara shook her head as she tried to calm her frantic

thoughts. Before she had been ashamed and worried that he might judge her humble little home if he saw it, but now it was much more than that. There was still shame, yes—but the overriding sense of shame was directed at her own appalling behaviour. She had behaved wantonly with a man she barely knew, displaying a fierce sexual hunger which was slightly terrifying. And Nikolai Komarov was the man who had made her feel that way. She didn't want another thing from him—and she certainly didn't want his driver reporting back where she lived.

Why not? questioned a rogue voice inside her head. *Are you afraid that if he turned up unexpectedly on your doorstep, you might not be able to turn him away?*

'I think we both know why,' she said quietly. 'We hardly know one another and we've just behaved in a way which was very…inappropriate.' She gazed into the ice-blue eyes and steeled herself against their sensual impact. 'And in view of that I think it's probably better if I make my own way home. It was nice to have met you…Nikolai.'

Stepping onto the pavement and taking a moment to steady herself on her high heels, Zara tugged down the silk-satin of her crumpled dress and turned to dart through a gate which led straight into the park, determined that this time he should not follow her.

For a moment Nikolai didn't move, frustration warring with admiration at her unexpected display of independence and feistiness and, yes, downright *prudishness.* She had walked away without taking his details and she had left him wanting more. *She had walked away.* He felt the drumming acceleration of his heart and the hot rush of blood to his groin. Now his hunter instincts were screaming to be satisfied and he slid his cell-phone from the pocket of his jacket and dialled up one of his aides.

Speaking rapidly in Russian, he clipped out the facts.

'Her name is Zara Evans,' he said, tasting her name as if her lips were still open beneath his, fingers of his free hand tapping impatiently against one hard, tense thigh. 'No, no—I don't know where she lives. In fact, I don't know a damned thing about her.' Except that he wanted her with a hunger he hadn't felt in a long time. A speculative smile curved the edges of his mouth as he stared up at the leather ceiling of the car. 'Just find her.'

CHAPTER THREE

ZARA picked up the tray of canapés and pinned her most professional smile to her lips as she and the other clutch of Gourmet International waitresses prepared to leave the vast kitchen. She glanced down to check that every grain of caviar was in place and that her tray contained a neat and snowy pile of napkins. Time to go out and flit between the guests. To be smooth and efficient. To top up glasses and whisk away discarded plates before they began to make the place look untidy.

The other waitresses were chatting as they made their way past priceless paintings which lined the corridor leading towards the gardens at the back of the house. But Zara wasn't in the mood for chatting, even though cocktail parties in private houses were usually her favourite kind of job. They were short enough not to allow boredom to creep in, they paid well—and were often held in the most luscious of locations. Like tonight. This was such a huge and beautiful setting that it was hard to believe that she was in the centre of London. But then, only the super-rich could afford to live in somewhere like Kensington Palace Gardens—a place which had been tagged by the envious as 'Billionaires' Row'. Only the favoured few waitresses had been chosen for such a plum job and the bonus payment should have given Zara cause to smile, but smiling wasn't coming very easily at the moment.

For days now, she'd been listless and distracted, her mind going round and round in circles. Preoccupied with the man who'd been haunting her dreams and waking hours ever since he'd taken her in his arms and made her body thrill to his experienced touch.

Nikolai Komarov. The icy-eyed Russian who had kissed her so passionately in the back of his luxury car after the embassy party last week. The man she had been trying desperately hard *not* to think about, but—no matter how much she tried to push the thoughts away— just the memory of the way he'd touched her made her heart hammer and her body ache.

Angrily, she straightened her shoulders. At least she should be grateful that there had been no repercussions after the event. Her friend's mum, her boss, hadn't found out that she'd gatecrashed the party—so at least her job was secure. She hadn't even told Emma about what had happened, she'd simply returned the dry-cleaned dress to her friend a couple of days later and told her that she'd been unable to get a card to the influential Russian billionaire. And that much was true. If she'd thrust a card at him after letting him kiss her like that, wouldn't it have looked like some primitive form of *barter*?

But the whole experience had left Zara feeling vulnerable—wondering how she could have behaved like that. Images of the intimate way he'd touched her kept coming back to haunt her with provocative clarity. She remembered the way his lips had sucked on her silk-covered breast. The way his fingers had drifted almost negligently over her bare leg. It had made her feel positively... *wanton*.

And added to her feelings of remorse was the financial

insecurity which was still looming large and ugly on the horizon. The bills which had accumulated during her godmother's illness still had to be paid. How on earth was she going to be able to honour them when waitressing paid so poorly and she was ill-equipped to be employed in any other capacity? Maybe she was going to have to sell the house after all, losing her toehold on the precious property market and at a time when prices were at an all-time low. Still, there was absolutely nothing she could do about it—at least, not tonight. She was here to do a job and so she had better just get out there and do it.

Resolutely putting her troubles to one side, she stepped out through tall French windows to the gardens, where she could see trees, bright flowerbeds, lawns and fountains. It looked more like an elegant public space than a private garden, she thought. Groups of people stood around in the warm summer evening—the women wearing pretty dresses and the men tieless and relatively casual. Waiters had already been circulating with chilled bottles of vintage champagne, and at the far end of the garden sat a woman with a fall of dark hair, who was playing gently on a harp.

'Crayfish wrapped in toasted-sesame rice and topped with golden caviar?' recited Zara as, with a smile, she offered her tray to group of bony-looking women in strappy little dresses—but they all shook their heads regretfully. Only the men accepted, devouring the costly treats in a careless mouthful, oblivious to the calorie-count they contained.

She moved from group to group, her smile not fading until she glanced to the end of the sunlit garden and saw a man standing there. She blinked and then blinked again, as if unable to believe what she was seeing. Because, standing perfectly still with his eyes trained on her, just as they had been when she'd first seen him, was Nikolai Komarov. Incredulity making her heart race, she registered the devastating combination of icy blue eyes, hair of beaten gold—and a body which was all honed muscular perfection.

Zara felt her feet stumble to a halt as she shook her head, thinking that she had simply imagined him, like someone who was parched from thirst imagining the gleam of water in the distance. Or perhaps the bright sunlight had blinded her to reality, making her think that because a man was tall and statuesque and stood as still as a waxwork it might be Nikolai Komarov.

But there could be no mistake. No other man looked like him. And no other man radiated that particular quality of power and domination...

She swallowed down the sudden lump in her throat as he began to walk across the grass towards her and she looked around her frantically, as if searching for some means of escape. But what could she do? Put her tray down on the lawn and run? And where could she run to in this enclosed garden, especially when at the very far end there were a couple of burly-looking security men, who didn't look as if they'd let anyone go anywhere without their boss's say-so?

She could see his face more closely now and his eyes looked so pale and cold that her heart began to hammer as he approached—and she could do absolutely nothing about the guilty prickle of her skin as her body acknowledged his devastating presence.

There was a pause before he spoke. A lifetime of a pause while he studied her with a look which managed to be both dispassionate and intense.

'Hello, Zara,' he said, in a voice edged with sensual danger.

For a moment she didn't reply, as if she still might wake up and find she had been dreaming. But he stood as solid as granite before her, as real as any man had a right to be, and she felt the rush of colour to her cheeks. 'Nikolai,' she breathed.

'The very same,' he agreed, clipping the words out as if they were bullets, his groin hardening as she said his name in that breathless way. And all he could think of was that she was nothing but a fraud, a liar and a cheat—just like the rest of her sex. It was ironic how predictable women could be. At first he'd thought that he'd just been scarred by a bad experience. That the template set down for him by his lying and cheating mother—who had walked away and left him without a backward glance—was somehow *unique*. But he had been wrong. After her desertion—the precious bond between mother and son forgotten in her pursuit of wealth—he had discovered a whole world of ambitious and deceitful women out there. His mouth twisted. When would he ever learn that they were all the same?

He fixed her with a cool look. 'Surprised?' he questioned sarcastically.

Her throat was still as dry as sandpaper. 'Of course I'm surprised,' she croaked. 'Why…why are you here? I don't…I don't understand. What's going on?'

Nikolai's eyes narrowed. He had been waiting for her, yes, but the reality of seeing her again still took some getting used to—especially when she looked so dramatically different. Tonight those pert breasts were not showcased by the slippery green satin which had drawn his mouth to them like a magnet—and nor was she towering and tall in a pair of sexy high heels. Instead, she was wearing a plain black skirt, white blouse and apron—an outfit which should have done her no favours at all. And yet somehow the functional uniform did little to disguise the lush curves of her body, drawing attention to every sinuous line of it. Or maybe that was because he had a good idea what lay beneath.

'Don't you?' He felt the breath thicken in his throat. 'No ideas at all?'

She shook her head, her confusion made worse by the explicit memory of his kisses. 'None.'

'Think about it.'

From jumbled fragments, the facts began to form some kind of picture in her mind. The only solution which made any kind of sense and yet one which filled her with foreboding as she thought about the possible repercussions. 'Is this…is this your house?'

'Bravo!' His lips curved into a mocking line. 'It's one of them. Do you like it?'

What could she say? Start protesting that her views on his property portfolio were irrelevant? Or just take the question at face-value and hope that her presence here was some kind of ghastly coincidence? 'It's a very beautiful house,' she said carefully.

'I know it is.' He gave a short laugh. 'I saw your reaction when you arrived.'

'You did?'

'Sure I did, *angel moy*. I was standing at my window when your minibus bumped its way up the drive. And I observed the look on your face as you jumped out.' It was a look he knew well. That wide-eyed look of awe and wistfulness. The look of someone dazzled by his vast wealth; who coveted it for themselves. Some called it greed, others called it envy—all Nikolai knew was that money changed everything. It made people do extraordinary things. Debase themselves. Sell out. Betray even the strongest of bonds and shatter them beyond recognition. It took the very best of human qualities and it twisted them inside out until they were black and unrecognisable. Didn't he know that—better than anyone?

Zara saw something dark and haunted pass over his shuttered features and a little shiver of dread began to whisper its way down her spine. 'Why am I here?' she whispered.

'Oh, come on—there's no need to make it sound like I'm preparing you for a human sacrifice.' He shrugged. 'It's simple. You're working for me. I specifically requested you. It's my party. Didn't anybody tell you?'

She shook her head. 'We aren't always told clients' names in advance—we weren't tonight.'

'Well, my cover is blown, *angel moy*—and now you do. I'm your client and you're working for me. You'll be serving food. Handing out drinks. Making sure my guests have everything they need. That *I* have everything I need. You know the drill—you're a waitress, aren't you? That's what you do. At least, that's what you do *some of the time*. I have to say that I'm a little puzzled about your real identity, or indeed about your motives— but now is not the time to discuss it. We'll have plenty of time for that later.'

His eyes glittered as they took in her trembling lips and he found that he wanted to crush them beneath his own in an angry kiss. And then? He pushed desire to the back of his mind. Desire could wait. His thick dark lashes lowered fractionally to reveal narrow shards of blue ice. 'I'm looking forward to getting to know you better, Zara.'

And with that final silky whisper, which sounded more like a threat, he walked away to a group who were standing beneath a flowering tree—leaving Zara staring after him in disbelief. Why had he *'specifically requested'* her, as he had put it—somehow managing to make her sound like some sort of commodity he'd purchased? *In fact, why had he brought her here at all?*

She realised that her tray needed replenishing, just as she realised that there was no means of escape—short of causing some kind of scene, which would heap dishonour not just on her, but on all the other staff. Nothing to do other than to carry on as she normally would and hope that he might give her some kind of reasonable explanation later. Yet even as she thought it she felt an overwhelming sense of unease, because Nikolai Komarov did not look like a man who did reasonable.

Trying to banish his image from her mind, she moved from guest to guest, wondering how she could endure a whole evening of having to stare into his impossibly handsome and mocking face. But as she continued to circulate she noticed that he barely glanced at her—and, ironically, Zara found this even worse.

Only once did she look up to meet his cold and imperious gaze and it felt like a lash of freezing rainwater flicked over her. She found herself swallowing down a growing sense of foreboding. Was he angry that she had pretended to be something she wasn't—that the woman he had kissed so passionately in his car was nothing more than a common little waitress? And yet, if she stopped to think about it, could she blame him? Just one glance at the women here who were hanging onto his every word showed that he usually mixed with supermodels and glossy heiresses. How shocked he must have been to have discovered who she really was!

By nine, most of the guests had left and Zara helped carry the last of the dirty dishes down to the kitchen.

The catering tonight had been especially lavish and the clearing up seemed to take much longer than usual—and yet she willed for it never to end. Surely Nikolai Komarov had something better to do than to hang around waiting for her to finish work? She went outside for one last check that everything was tidy to find the garden deserted and she gave a sigh of relief.

She had just retrieved a champagne glass from one of the flowerbeds and was heading back into the house when she saw Nikolai walking out onto the terrace and Zara's footsteps faltered to a halt. Had he seen her? He had removed his jacket to reveal a soft shirt of snowy silk and the top two buttons of the shirt were unbuttoned, revealing an enticing V of bare flesh—but the casual look made him no less formidable.

She felt her mouth drying as she stared up at the sensual curve of his lips and the icy gleam of his eyes. Yes, he had seen her.

'So who exactly are you?' he questioned as his footsteps brought him to a halt in front of her.

'You know who I am. I told you. Zara Evans.'

'*Net.*' Impatiently, he shook his head and gave an imperious wave of his hand, as if he were swatting away some imaginary fly. 'Your name may or may not have changed—but you certainly have done.' His gaze flicked to the sturdy black shoes she wore with her uniform. 'You'll agree that you represent a rather dramatic fall from grace—from riches to rags within days?'

'No. There are no riches. The rags are the real me.' She bit her lip—as if suddenly becoming aware of the huge disparity between their two lives and the risk she had taken in pretending that she was his equal. How stupid could she have been? 'I'm really a waitress.'

'As I was to discover for myself.'

'How? How did you find out?'

Cynically, Nikolai's mouth hardened. Didn't she realise that there wasn't any information in the world which
was off-limits if you had the money to pay someone
to play detective? Tracking down a waitress had been
child's play.

'That part was easy—you can find anyone you want
if you have the means,' he drawled. 'But what I really
want to know is why you were masquerading as a guest
at the ambassador's party. Why you played that erotic
hide-and-seek which had me following you like a puppy-
dog.' And he had fallen right into it, hadn't he? Lids half
hooding his eyes, he watched closely for her reaction.
Was she a celebrity stalker? he wondered. One of those
women who fixed a wealthy man in their sights and
pursued him? What did she want from him? 'Were you
deliberately targeting me?'

Zara's heart gave a guilty lurch. Would it sound stupid
if she told him that, *yes*, she had been looking out for
him, but that the motive had been nothing but an innocent bit of advertising? And then things had all got
out of hand—when she had seen him and danced with
him and that sizzling chemistry had combusted between
them. Would he believe her or think that she was lying?
Think that she put out like that all the time? Play for
time, she told herself. Find out the kind of man you're
dealing with. 'Why should I want to target you?'

'Please don't be disingenuous,' he warned, and as he
saw the rise in colour to her cheeks he knew she was
hiding something. 'Powerful men are subjected to all
kinds of come-ons from women—some cleverer than
others. Usually I can see through them, but your ap-
proach was novel.' And sexy, he conceded. She had made
him chase her. For once, he'd felt the thrill of the hunt,

the blood pumping hotly through his veins as he'd followed the silken curves of her bottom.

His reaction had taken him aback. It had been a primitive, subliminal response and it had been inordinately compelling. Why, hadn't the thought of finding her again filled him with a heady kind of anticipation—until he had discovered her true identity and suspected that he might be the victim of some kind of crude scam? 'I want the truth,' he snapped. 'Or is that too big an ask?'

Zara saw the glitter of danger which was hardening his eyes and realised that she was doing herself no favours by being evasive.

'Okay. I had no right to be at the party—at least, not as a guest,' she admitted. 'I gatecrashed it—though I knew most of the waitresses, obviously, since I work with them most of the time. I was modelling the dress for a friend of mine, Emma. Her mother owns the catering agency I work for. That's how she knew who was going to be on the guest-list.'

His expression didn't alter. 'Go on.'

'Emma's a fashion student—and she's very ambitious.'

He frowned. 'A fashion student?'

'That's right. She's good at designing evening gowns and she wanted a bit of exposure.'

'Exposure being the operative word,' he drawled. 'You certainly left very little to the imagination.'

Something in his tone brought another rush of colour to Zara's cheeks. 'The dress I was wearing was no more revealing than plenty of others there.'

But no other woman in the room had possessed her firm and slinky young body, Nikolai remembered with a sudden ache. Whatever it was she had, it had appealed to him on a very fundamental level. It still did. Even the drab knee-length skirt and innocuous white blouse she was wearing tonight were doing dangerous things to his blood pressure. *Remember that she's nothing but a fraud,* he told himself. *And that all women are frauds.*

'So what exactly was your brief?' he demanded.

'I was supposed to give you one of her business cards.'

'Hoping that I'd play fairy godfather and give her the big break she deserved?' he questioned sarcastically.

'Something like that.'

'But you didn't, did you?' he said thoughtfully. 'So what happened, Zara? Did you decide to jettison that idea when something better came along? Did you think that by capitalising on the undoubted chemistry between us you could aim even higher than a mere marketing opportunity?' He raised his eyebrows in a mocking question. 'Maybe you thought that if you could get your claws into me, then you might benefit far more than just getting a cut from the sale of your friend's clothes?'

'What a cynic you are,' she breathed.

'It comes with the territory,' he snapped.

Zara stared at him in distress. 'You seem to forget that *I* was the one who terminated the evening.'

'Ah, but not before you'd given me a taste of your spectacular love-making,' he said thoughtfully. 'Was that to set my blood on fire, my beauty? To tantalise me and leave me wanting more? Because I have to tell you that you succeeded.'

She shook her head. 'If that had been the case then why would I just disappear from your car?'

He shrugged. 'Perhaps you were biding your time, knowing that a man who has everything will be tantalised by the thrill of the chase?' He gave a short and cynical laugh. 'I know how devious women can be.'

'Well, you're wrong,' Zara said, wondering if he had had his heart badly broken by someone and if that was the reason for the bitterness which had distorted his voice. 'Completely wrong. I found events running away with me in a way I hadn't planned and I knew I needed to get away from there. From you.'

There was silence for a moment until the sweet notes of a nightingale pierced the air and Zara suddenly realised that it was dark.

'I'm not sure whether or not I believe you,' he said at last.

There was a pause. 'Well, that's your prerogative,' she answered, hiding the hurt which rushed through her and feeling like a child who had been wrongly accused of stealing. 'But it's irrelevant now surely—and all in the past. I wasn't out to try to extract some of your precious fortune from you—so can I please go now?'

But as Nikolai's gaze rested on her parted lips he suddenly realised that he didn't care what her motives were. Did it matter if she was a liar or a cheat? The bottom line was that he still wanted her—it was nothing more complicated than that. Inexplicably, he *really* wanted her. To lose himself in her kiss again and to feel that incredible body wrapped close against his. In fact, he was tempted to start making love to her right now and rid himself of the fever which burned so hotly in his veins. To find some quiet and private corner where he could thrust deep inside her, while the warm and scented summer air surrounded them and she cried her pleasure against his neck.

Yet Nikolai knew that timing was everything. And now was not the right time. Not when she was convincing herself that she'd been hard done by and her face had adopted that proud and stubborn little look which made

him think that he might have to kiss her into submission.
Or maybe she might even just turn him down again. Was
she feisty enough to try? He suspected she was.

His heart give a sudden urgent beat of expectation.
Why opt for a clandestine coupling at the end of an evening? Why not enjoy her at his leisure—and satisfy himself in the process that, like all women, she was driven
by nothing more complicated than greed, no matter how
strong the attraction which burned between them?

'No, don't go yet,' he said softly. 'You see, I have a
proposition to put to you.'

Zara eyed him warily. 'A p-proposition?'

'That's right. How would you like to come and work
for me in my villa in the South of France?'

Uncomprehendingly, she stared at him. 'You mean
as a waitress?'

He bit back a cynical laugh. What did she imagine—
that he was asking her to act as his hostess? His partner
for the weekend? 'Of course. I always need staff and I'm
having a very small, very casual house-party. Often I
just use people from the nearby village—but you speak
English. Any other languages?' He wasn't surprised
when she shook her head. 'No? Well, that's precisely
what I want. You could be useful.'

Useful? 'Why?' she questioned slowly.

'I have a Russian colleague who likes to do business when nobody around can understand what he's
saying.'

Zara frowned as she tried to make sense of his offer.
'I didn't mean that—I mean, why me? Why offer me the
job?'

His icy eyes mocked her. He was finding a way to
see her again, surely she realised that—or was she playing another game by pretending she didn't? 'Are you in

the habit of quizzing prospective employers about their objectives?'

'Obviously, it's slightly different in your case.'

'Obviously,' he echoed sardonically. 'You're one of the best waitresses around, aren't you? At least, that's what I was told when I booked through your company for this party. That's reason enough. And of course, I pay well. Very well.' Softly, he mentioned a sum and saw her eyes widen, saw the pink tip of her tongue snake out to run its way over her lips, and he felt a powerful mix of disdain and desire. How exquisitely avaricious she was, he thought—and that realisation was curiously liberating. He need not be troubled by his conscience, he thought—for she clearly wasn't. 'So what do you think, Zara—do you think I could persuade you to take the job?'

Zara hesitated, unbearably tempted by the amount of money he was offering. Why, a sum like that would write off most of her debts. Would allow her to shake off the burden of responsibility which weighed so heavily on her shoulders. Would mean that she could start living like a normal twenty-something instead of someone who was worried sick about the future and all it entailed. Wouldn't she be out of her mind to turn down an opportunity like that? Even if it meant working for a man who made her skin shiver with desire?

'When is it?' she questioned.

'Next weekend.'

'But that's the weekend I'm...' Her voice trailed off as she thought about the date with a sweet but unexciting man which Emma had lined up for her.

'The weekend you're what?' he prompted.

'I was supposed to be...seeing someone.'

'Ah.' Idly, he wondered who the poor fool was. 'Then

take a rain check. Work comes first.' His mouth hardened. 'Happens to me all the time.'

Temptation washed over her in a renewed wave, yet still Zara hesitated. She might be naïve about certain aspects of the world, but she certainly wasn't stupid and she knew perfectly well that Nikolai Komarov's offer wasn't as straightforward as it seemed.

Because he wanted her. She knew that, too. She could sense the sexual hunger which shimmered off his powerful frame—matching a need which burned deep inside *her*. Could she really go and work for him, knowing all that?

She lifted her eyes to his, remembering all the women he was reputed to have dated and cast aside, and she felt the stir of challenge. Couldn't she be strong enough to resist him if he came onto her? As strong as she'd been for her godmother—though in a different way? Surely it couldn't be difficult to keep at arm's length a man who treated women with such little regard as he did. Especially when he was presenting her with the opportunity to ease all her financial woes.

'Okay. I'll do the job,' she said slowly.

Nikolai nodded and felt the slow beat of inevitability. Of course she would. Of course she would cancel whatever it was she was supposed to be doing. She'd probably let down some poor idiot who was slavering to see her. Because whoever she was supposed to be seeing wouldn't stand a chance when measured next to what *he* could offer. His mouth twisted. Nikolai was used to people falling in with his wishes, but that didn't stop him sometimes praying that they wouldn't. That for once the lure of his money would fail to procure the prize. And that, he knew, was like wishing for the stars which glittered so coldly in the night sky above them. 'Excellent,' he breathed.

'Just...' She met his eyes and sucked in a lungful of air as he raised his eyebrows in arrogant question. 'Just as long as you understand that...well, what happened the night of the party was a mistake. A big mistake—and one I have no intention of repeating. You do know that? That this is simply a professional arrangement.'

With difficulty, Nikolai bit back a laugh at the outrageousness of this little chit of a waitress laying down her conditions to a man like him. *As if she meant a single word of it!* Didn't she realise that he could see the points of her nipples as they pushed against her white shirt, in flagrant and silent invitation? Why were women so fundamentally dishonest about their needs and their desires? he wondered bitterly. She wanted him just as much as he wanted her—and surely she must realise that chemistry like this was too potent to squander? 'If that is what you want,' he murmured, 'then I give you my word that is what you shall get, *angel moy.*'

He felt not one shred of remorse as he uttered the empty words and saw her nod in response, a misplaced look of trust settling on her features.

His mouth hardened as he turned away. Because promises were made to be broken. Hadn't that been one of the very first lessons he'd learned in life when he was scarcely out of the cradle?

CHAPTER FOUR

'AND this,' said the housekeeper, opening the door with a flourish, 'is your room.'

Blinking back her surprise, Zara followed the woman inside—because the small apartment wasn't what she'd been expecting. Normally, waitresses were allocated rooms which would give a prison cell a run for its money—but not here. It seemed that even the staff accommodation in Nikolai Komarov's south of France villa was luxurious. A big bed dazzled with snowy linen, there was a kitchen, an amazing bathroom—as well as shuttered windows which looked out onto a breathtaking view of the misty Provençal mountains in the distance.

'This looks wonderful,' she said slowly, her gaze drifting to a heap of black grapes which gleamed in a bowl as if they were waiting for an artist to paint them.

'Yes, well—Mr Komarov always looks after his staff,' said the housekeeper crisply. 'He just expects hard work and discretion in return. Now I'll leave you to get changed—you'll be serving lunch within the hour. I hope the whistle-stop tour of the house didn't confuse you? No? Good. Then come straight to the kitchens when you're ready.'

Zara put her little overnight bag down on the floor and gave a bright smile. 'Will do.'

At least the housekeeper's words reminded her that she was here to work and, once the woman had gone, Zara stripped out of her travelling clothes and took a quick shower. The water on her skin felt delicious but the faint misgivings she'd felt since accepting this job simply wouldn't go away.

She'd asked herself over and over again whether she'd been right to come here and put herself at the mercy of the powerful and sexy Russian. But there hadn't really been any choice, had there? Not in the end.

Any second thoughts she might have had about agreeing to Nikolai's offer had been swiftly quashed when a whole new raft of bills had arrived. Zara had opened up the brown envelopes, seen the bold red print screaming out at her—and there, sitting incongruously among all the final demands, had been a first-class air-ticket to Nice. She'd picked it up and studied it with a terrible sense of inevitability, knowing there was no way she could afford to turn down the kind of money he was proposing to pay her.

So she'd taken the plane from Heathrow and tried to quell her rising nerves, but it hadn't been easy, especially when disturbing images of his cold face and hard body kept drifting into her mind. At Nice, a car had been waiting to drive her through the hairpin bends of the Corniche—with its stunning green mountains on one side, dropping dramatically down to sapphire sea on the other. And when she'd arrived at Nikolai's villa it had been like stepping into something you saw between the glossy pages of lifestyle magazines.

The vast gardens were a picture of cascading fountains and curving paths, while flowers in every shade imaginable dazzled the eye. At the end of the long drive was the house itself, a building which dwarfed every other she'd ever seen. Coloured a beautiful pale rose, it stood contrasted against the magnificence of the mountains behind, and offered breathtaking views of the glittering Côte d'Azure.

Turning off the shower, Zara towelled herself dry and pulled on a clean uniform, telling herself that the lavish beauty of Nikolai's world was irrelevant. And so was the fact that she found him overwhelmingly attractive. She was here to work and walk away with a hefty pay-cheque, and she'd better not forget that.

Going straight to the kitchens, she checked timings with the chef and had just carried a bottle of vintage champagne up to the terrace when she heard the sound of footsteps behind her. Fingers tightening around the cold silver ice bucket, she felt her heart skip a beat, because instinct told her that Nikolai Komarov was right behind her.

Act like you normally would if he were any other employer. Smile politely and say hello. But her legs felt wobbly as she slowly turned round, her heart now crashing against her ribcage as his cool gaze washed over her.

There was nothing of the billionaire about Nikolai Komarov today. He was wearing the kind of off-duty clothes worn by men the world over, be they billionaire or student, but Zara doubted whether anybody had ever looked as good in them as he did. Faded blue jeans skated over the narrow jut of his hips and skimmed down over the hard, muscular legs. A simple black T-shirt moulded his lean torso and the short sleeves showed off powerful forearms, his tanned skin looking as if it had been dusted with flecks of gold.

Meeting the mockery in his ice-blue eyes, she swallowed and tried to control breathing which had suddenly become shallow and erratic. Why had she stupidly discounted how gorgeous he was? As if a few days' distance might have given her some kind of magical immunity to him. *Well, she was going to have to acquire some—and quickly!* Somehow she found her voice. 'Good morning, Mr Komarov.'

'Oh, please.' His eyes gleamed sardonically as he took in the tremble of her lips. 'I think we know each other well enough to dispense with unnecessary formality, don't you? It's quite acceptable for you to call me Nikolai when we are alone.'

Zara's polite smile didn't slip. 'If that's what you want.'

He thought that now wasn't the moment to tell her exactly what he wanted—even if she *did* sound deliciously compliant. How huge her green eyes looked as they studied him, he mused. All startled and bright, yet somehow managing to be both wary and yearning all at the same time. 'You know, I half expected you not to show up,' he observed. 'To have decided that this job might be a little more than you can handle.'

'But we came to a professional agreement,' she defended.

'And the money was too good to turn your back on?'

'There is that, of course.' Her eyes were very steady as she looked at him because she was damned if she would let him make her feel bad about needing the money. What would *he* know about pinching and scraping and trying to get creditors off your back? 'And I'm not in the habit of letting people down.'

'I'm impressed,' he murmured, noticing the almost imperceptible elevation of her chin and hearing the sudden note of pride which had entered her voice.

'That wasn't my intention.'

'No?'

'No,' she answered. 'I'm simply here to do a job and to do it to the best of my ability.'

And judging by her appearance, it occurred to him that she might be speaking the truth—because she didn't look as he had been expecting her to look. Hadn't he thought she might play the vamp? For her hair to be tumbling in provocative tendrils around her face and her skirt suddenly to have shrunk by a couple of sizes? Something more befitting her status as the kind of woman who was out for everything she could get than a lowly little waitress. But she looked nothing like that. He frowned. Her face was almost bare of make up, her hair was tugged back into a functional ponytail—and surely an off-duty nun would have found no fault in the respectable length of her dull black skirt.

And wasn't it ironic that her very lack of adornment was only increasing his desire for her instead of diminishing it? So that for a moment he felt irritated that he couldn't just pull her into his arms and kiss her and have done with it. That he was going to have to endure this charade of her waiting at his table in order to bed her. Reluctantly, he elevated his gaze to her face.

'You look very…professional—although your uniform isn't the most alluring I've ever seen,' he remarked as, with another kick of surprise, he noted her soft rise of colour. 'And now I've made you blush.'

His comment made her colour deepen even more. 'I blush at the drop of a hat,' she admitted.

'Really?' He slanted her a mocking glance. 'And yet I didn't really have you down as the shy, retiring type.'

Zara remembered the way she'd responded to him in the back of his car—like some kind of insatiable man-eater, devouring his lips and letting him suckle on her breasts when they'd only just met. Could she blame him if he'd leapt to the wrong conclusion about her? Feeling wrong-footed and with no way of defending herself, Zara heard the sound of approaching footsteps with a sigh of relief.

'No time to stand around chatting,' she said hurriedly. 'I think your guests are about to make an appearance. I'd better go and start opening the champagne.'

His gaze held hers and in that moment he silently cursed his guests. 'I suppose you must,' he said reluctantly.

Zara reached for the champagne bottle as if it were a lifeline. Why the hell was he giving her that sexy sizzle of a stare? Hadn't he heard her when she'd told him in London that this was going to be a purely professional engagement—or did men like him simply ride rough-shod over someone else's wishes if they didn't happen to coincide with their own? And if that was the case, how the hell was she going to deal with it when she found him so completely irresistible? When part of her *wanted* him to tease her and mock her like that, while sexual tension fizzed in the air around them.

Tearing gold foil from the bottle and easing out the cork with a quiet pop, she saw a couple walk out onto the terrace and began to study them with covert interest. She'd wondered what Nikolai's house guests might be like—but this mismatched pair weren't at all what she'd been expecting.

The man was short, rotund and aged about fifty and, despite his loose linen clothes, kept dabbing at his damp neck with a linen handkerchief. But it was his girlfriend who was the eye-catcher. She was about three decades younger than him, and wore red patent shoes which made her tower over her companion. A waterfall of blonde hair fell to her tiny waist and sawn-off denim hot-pants emphasised her long, tanned legs. She looked as if he'd picked her out of a catalogue, thought Zara. And in her plain A-line black skirt and flat shoes, she suddenly felt like a complete frump in comparison.

Nikolai lifted his hand in greeting. 'Sergei—I can't believe that I've prised you away from the attractions of Paris! Aren't you already having withdrawal symptoms?'

'Invitations to Paradis are too rare to ever be refused,' laughed the man. 'Though I guess you must be eager for a fellow Muscovite to confide in! Nobody sees the world in quite the same way as a Russian.'

'Ah, but you must know by now that I confide in no one.'

'No, I've heard you play your cards very close to your chest,' gushed the blonde, and Nikolai raised his eyebrows.

'I don't believe we've met?' he said.

'No, wc haven't. I'm Crystal,' said the blonde. 'And you're Nikolai. Mmm. Suddenly I can understand why all my girlfriends went green when I told them where I was staying!' Her glossy lips sparkled in the sunlight. 'God, we got stuck in a pig of a traffic jam outside Monte Carlo and I'm absolutely parched—can I have a drink before I pass out?'

Nikolai gave a cool smile. Perhaps her skills in the bedroom compensated for her apparent lack of social graces, he thought caustically as he gestured towards Zara. 'Of course you can. Champagne okay for you?'

'Mmm! I love champagne!'

'I rather thought you might,' observed Nikolai drily.

'Well, why don't we sit over here and enjoy the gardens—lunch won't be long, will it, Zara?'

'No, sir,' she answered, her cheeks even redder now as she listened to Crystal's shameless flirting. No wonder Nikolai thought all women had some kind of agenda.

With a dexterity borne of countless jobs, Zara kept their glasses topped up and soon began serving the deceptively simple lunch which had been prepared. She busied around with the seafood salad, making sure that Sergei's glass was topped up with copious amounts of bourbon, which was the only thing he drank, but all the time she was listening to their conversation—at least, what she could understand of it.

Nikolai and Sergei kept breaking into bursts of Russian—while Crystal said, or ate, very little. In fact, the blonde spent most of the meal holding out her champagne glass to be filled up and moodily staring out at the distant glitter of the Mediterranean.

What must it be like for a woman to be ignored like that? Zara wondered as she served the dessert, a pale yellow *tarte au citron*. Didn't Crystal mind that she was being treated like an ornament—or was that the price she paid for being brought to exquisite places like this? She was so lost in her thoughts that for a moment she didn't notice the mocking blue gaze which was being angled in her direction, until she looked up and was caught in the cool crossfire of Nikolai's gaze. *Please don't let me blush again*, she thought. *Don't let him realise that he's getting under my skin*. For a split second his eyes were thoughtful as they skimmed over her and, beneath her thin white cotton shirt, she could feel the heated prickle of her skin.

'We'll have coffee now, Zara,' he instructed softly.

She nodded, her throat feeling thick and dry. 'Certainly, sir. Shall I serve it out here?'

'If you would.'

It was an exchange she'd had countless times in her working life but for once Zara found it hard not to resent her subservient status as she hurried off to the kitchen. Having to wear a too-hot skirt and apron and to sweat slightly beneath the too-heavy weight of the coffee tray as she made her way back to the terrace. Having to fade into the background as if she were a ghost rather than a real person.

Was that because she'd had a brief taste of what Nikolai's life was like—tasted it and liked it—and wasn't that dangerous? So stop thinking about it, she told herself fiercely as she slid a chilled plate of truffles onto the table.

Nikolai watched as she bent to pour him coffee and noticed the tiny pinpoints of sweat which were beading her pale brow. Through the cheap white blouse she wore, he could make out the outline of a bra which looked more functional than decorative. His eyes drifted to the appalling, heavy-soled black shoes. And suddenly, he felt bemused. There were a million women who could be his at the snap of a finger—so what was it about this little creature which had so captured his imagination? Surely now that he had seen her for what she really was—a waitress and not a goddess—then his hunger for her would wane and he could forget all about her.

So why the hell did he feel an aching throb of frustration whenever he looked at her?

Crystal suddenly stood up, and gave a rather theatrical yawn. 'Well, I'm off to sunbathe—anyone else fancy joining me? Sergei—are you coming?'

'No, not now.' Shaking his head, Sergei withdrew a phone from his pocket. 'I have to talk business.'

Crystal turned her head to look at her host and her smile changed. 'How about you, Nikolai?'

Nikolai realised that the blonde was gleaming him a hungry look. Now *this* was a textbook predator, he thought as he shook his head. Some glossy accessory of a woman who wore her rich lover's jewels and then flirted with his younger and more virile associate. Not some pale-faced waitress who hadn't put a foot wrong since she'd been here.

He watched as Zara piled another set of dishes on her loaded tray and another unexpected stab of conscience hit him. Had he misjudged her? Did he only want her because she had misled him—so that his resulting anger had provided an extra frisson to the sexual hunger he already felt for her? Surely that was the only *logical* explanation?

'When you've finished clearing away you can go, Zara,' he said abruptly. 'Just be back to serve cocktails at seven—okay? But until then, you're free.'

Zara thought how shuttered his face had suddenly become and that there were no traces of lazy sensuality being directed at her now. In fact, he was behaving exactly as an employer *should* behave—dismissing her in that slightly curt manner which seemed to emphasise the differences in their status. And if she was experiencing a sudden pang of disappointment because that brief intimacy between them had faded, then she should be ashamed of herself. She gave a little nod. 'Thank you, sir.'

Back in her room, Zara pulled off her hot uniform and hung it in the wardrobe with a sigh of relief. She had come through her first test unscathed and now she had a free afternoon ahead of her. How free was free? she wondered as she splashed cold water onto her face. Free enough to slip on a pair of shorts and to wander around this Mediterranean paradise of his?

But there were unspoken rules in her job. You merged into the background and became invisible. You certainly didn't sunbathe in the grounds of a client's mansion, no matter how extensive they might be. Imagine the embarrassment of being discovered sprawled out, half naked and covered in suncream! Instead, she opened up the guidebook she'd bought at the airport that morning and saw that there was a picturesque little village close enough for her to reach by foot. Her eyes scanned the tempting photos as she read up about St Jean Gardet— one of those tiny, magical places up in the mountains, which looked as if it hadn't changed for decades.

No one except the man at the main security gates saw her as she slipped out of the grounds and felt the warm breeze on her face as she set off. She walked upwards through the scented hills, hearing nothing other than the occasional bleat of a goat or the whispery buzz of crickets—and was hot and thirsty by the time she reached the tiny village.

The place seemed to have gone to sleep for the afternoon because there didn't seem to be a soul around. It was a beautiful ghost town of a place, with scarlet geraniums tumbling from window boxes. A dog slept beneath the shade of a tree and the clock chimed loudly in the baking square. Eventually she found a small *tabac* where a woman dressed in black looked at her with suspicious eyes and effected not to understand Zara's schoolgirl attempts at French. But she bought herself a bottle of water and gulped it down thirstily before setting off to explore the cool interior of the small church which was at the very heart of the village.

Afterwards, she felt refreshed by the experience and set off back towards the road leading to Nikolai's villa—telling herself that she was lucky to be able to explore such a gorgeous place. All she had to do was to endure a few more meals before walking away with her more-than-generous pay-cheque. She could get rid of her debts and then she really *would* be free. Free to start thinking about what she was going to do with the rest of her life. And if a part of her heart was wistful at the thought that she would never see the sexy Russian again, common sense told her that it was by far the best thing.

Unfortunately, the journey back to the villa seemed much hotter and dustier. Sweat trickled down from her neck to lay in a clammy film on her back and she kept pushing heavy strands of hair away from her face and wondering when she would see Nikolai's estate. She was so lost in her thoughts that at first she didn't register the distant drone of an engine—not until the drone became a throaty roar and she realised that a car was speeding down the mountain road towards her.

Quickly, she stepped back onto a verge massed with tall grass and wild flowers as a powerful silver sports car streaked by, gleaming like a fish in the bright sunlight. Dust like golden smoke clouded up behind as it shot past.

With a skipped beat of her heart, she registered the hard profile of the driver. She saw the wind whipping through hair the colour of beaten gold. For a moment the vehicle slowed as the driver glanced in his rear mirror, before slamming on his brakes. The car came to a screaming halt a little way down the road, before being reversed up with an arrogant skill to stop right beside her.

Zara thought that if he hadn't been a billionaire entrepreneur, then Nikolai Komarov could easily have been a racing driver. Her heart was thudding so loudly that it seemed to deafen her as she stared down into eyes which were hidden by dark shades.

His mouth gave the hint of a hard smile as he leaned over and pushed open the door.

'Get in,' he said.

CHAPTER FIVE

ZARA stared down into Nikolai's sculpted features, but he was wearing wrap-around shades and so it was impossible to see his eyes or properly see his expression.

'Get in the car,' he repeated impatiently.

'I'm enjoying the walk.'

'Maybe you were—but not any more, I think. You're hot. Or at least you look it,' he added.

She could feel the heat in her cheeks and the stickiness of her skin beneath her sundress and as he spoke she could feel another slow trickle of sweat as it meandered down her back. He was right—she was absolutely baking—but surely getting into a car with him was the worst possible solution. Yet wouldn't it look slightly pathetic if she refused his offer of a lift—especially when they were both heading for the same place? And what about all those little pep talks she'd been giving herself about managing to resist him? 'Okay.' She gave a little shrug and a small smile. 'Why not? Thanks.'

Sliding into the low leather seat, she attempted to swing her legs into the car without showing too much flesh, but it wasn't easy—especially when she was feeling this self-conscious and knowing that he was watching her. He waited until she'd snapped her seat belt on and then started the engine.

'So where have you been?' he questioned as the car pulled away.

'Exploring. My guidebook said St Jean Gardet was especially beautiful.'

'And did you agree with your guidebook?'

Zara shrugged. 'Well, it was certainly very pretty—but the woman in the shop wasn't particularly friendly towards me.'

'The locals are very protective, that's all. We get a lot of strange visitors to the area—journalists looking for a scoop or thieves doing a little prep-work.'

'I hadn't thought of that.' Zara risked a glance at his profile, at the golden gleam of his skin and the soft shadows which fell beneath his high cheekbones. She supposed that when you were as wealthy as he was, you must necessarily view every new acquaintance with suspicion. A pang of guilt ran through her as she remembered her own behaviour the night of the party. Perhaps she couldn't blame him for being so wary. 'Otherwise, it was very quiet—there didn't seem to be anyone else around.'

'Well, what do you expect? It's four-thirty in the afternoon, when the day is at its hottest.' He shot her a glance. 'Anyone with any sense would be sheltered inside, in the cool.'

'Having a siesta?' she said, keen to show him that she did know *something* about a southern European lifestyle.

'Maybe.' His mouth quirked into the flicker of a smile. 'Though I can think of far better alternatives for whiling away an afternoon than merely sleeping, can't you, Zara?'

Zara kept her eyes fixed steadily ahead. She had

walked straight into *that* one, hadn't she? 'Yet strangely, you're out in the sun yourself,' she said.

'Maybe that's because I don't have anyone offering me a little afternoon delight, *milaya moya*. Something which might tempt me into staying home.'

Zara's cheeks grew even hotter. Afternoon delight meant…well, everyone knew what it meant. He was trying to embarrass her, that was for sure—and she was not going to give him the pleasure of succeeding. 'I'm sure that can't be true, Nikolai. Someone like you must be besieged with offers from women all the time.'

'Oh, I am,' he agreed gravely. 'But you know…' there was a pause as he negotiated a hairpin bend '…if something is offered to you on a plate, then it sometimes deadens the appetite.'

'Yet you ate most of your lunch, I noticed,' she observed innocently.

At this, he gave an unexpected laugh and behind the concealment of his shades his eyes narrowed. She was brighter than he had thought. Much brighter. Not that it mattered, of course. Her intelligence was not the reason he wanted her. 'So I did,' he agreed smoothly. 'Perhaps I found the meal irresistible because it had been served by your own fair hand.'

'Or perhaps because you employ a world-class chef to cook it for you?'

He felt the sudden beat of his heart, because her sparring was turning him on almost as much as the silky-pale knees exposed by her cheap little dress. 'Perhaps.'

'And where have *you* been driving to?' she questioned curiously.

Nikolai's mouth hardened into a grim smile. He'd popped out to his wine merchant in a nearby town. When he'd seen her as he drove back, the closest thing he had to a conscience had told him that maybe he should just leave her alone. That she had worked hard during lunch and made no attempt whatsoever to flirt with him. In fact, she had a strange kind of innocence about her and he suspected it would be wrong to make love to her.

But her ripe young body and the tremulous parting of her fleshy lips were fast drawing a veil over his reluctant reservations. He wanted to kiss her and he wanted it badly. And she, he suspected, wanted it just as much.

'I've just been to see my friend who delivers my wine for me. And giving the car a run in the process. I'm away so much that it sits idling in the garage for much of the time.'

'Oh.' In the distance, she caught a glimpse of his pale rose mansion and knew they couldn't be that far from his estate. And suddenly, she felt a sense of disappointment that this sunlit car ride was going to come to an end. Did she communicate something of that disappointment to him—and was that why he shot her another swift glance?

'Do you want to see something beautiful?' he questioned suddenly.

Zara hesitated. But she had handled him okay so far, hadn't she? Had refused to react to his murmured little innuendos and had somehow remained calm. And when would she ever get another chance like this—to see the beautiful south of France through an insider's eyes?

'Yes, please.'

He drove the car around several more bends, before bringing it to a smooth halt on a natural rocky viewing point, which jutted out from the winding road. 'Take a look at that,' he said softly.

For a moment Zara said nothing as she gazed down at bright turquoise sea which glittered in the afternoon sunlight. The little coves which edged it were fringed with fine silver sand and there were green lines of parasol pines which looked like giant umbrellas. It was so beautiful that for a moment she struggled to find words which would do it justice. 'Oh, it's amazing,' she breathed. 'So…so *blue*—and there's so *much* of it.'

'The area is on a natural peninsula,' said Nikolai. 'Which is why the water seems to surround us. We have some of the best beaches along the Côte d'Azure—but we don't have the massive tourist influx of Nice and Cannes, and we're only a short drive from Italy.'

'You sound like you're selling real estate.'

'Oh, believe me—I've done that before,' he commented wryly.

She stared down at the sea—at the darker shades of rippling sapphire where the waters grew deeper. And she tried to imagine somebody actually living with this kind of beauty—waking up and seeing it every morning for the rest of their lives, if they wanted to. 'You're very lucky,' she said, without thinking.

The word 'lucky' jolted Nikolai from his guided tour and brought reality crashing in like the waves on the rocks below. For a moment he forgot the fact that her hair gleamed like gold and that her sun-warmed body was just crying out to be touched. *Lucky.* He swallowed a bitter laugh. That was what people always said. What they always presumed about him when they saw the houses and the cars and the priceless antiques in the properties he had dotted around the globe. How he hated the word with all its random associations. As if he had been bestowed with precious gifts at birth—handed wealth and privilege—when nothing could be further from the truth. Sometimes he wondered what the reaction might be if he came right out and told it as it really was.

Was it 'lucky' to be abandoned like a feral animal and left to fend for yourself? And then to discover that you meant nothing to the woman who had given birth to you? That the supposedly most powerful bond of love which existed between mother and child had as much substance as a puff of smoke.

His mouth hardened as forbidden memories broke free like black clouds which swarmed into his mind and darkened it. Until he reminded himself that bitterness was a waste of time and energy. It had all turned out right for him in the end, hadn't it? Even if the price he had paid had been an inability to trust anyone ever again. He couldn't change the past—nobody could—but he could capitalise on the present and enjoy it. Because a man had to make his own luck in life…

'Do you know that, right now, I feel like the luckiest person in the world,' he said softly.

Unable to stop herself, Zara slowly turned her head to look at him, even though she knew that he was probably spinning her a line. Just as she knew he was going to kiss her and she wasn't going to lift a finger to stop him. Because who could fail to be captivated by the sea and the sunlight, the fragrant air and the sensual softening of Nikolai's lips? Wasn't this one of those perfect moments which stayed in your mind for ever, no matter what happened afterwards? 'So do I,' she said truthfully.

He felt the wild kick of desire as he pulled her into his arms, remembering that she felt even better than she looked. All warm and soft and instantly accessible—with her windswept hair loose and spilling over her shoulders in silken disarray. With his thumb he traced the outline of her lips and when they began to tremble he bent his head and claimed them with his own.

The kiss was hard and urgent and a powerful jerk

of desire arrowed through him as he inhaled her scent of roses and suncream. They kissed until there was no breath left and he pulled away from her, trying to regain some of the customary control which had momentarily deserted him.

'I've been wanting to do that to you all day,' he said unevenly.

'Ha-have you?'

'You know damned well I have. And more. Much more. Shall I show you how much?'

'No.' Her tongue snaked out over her lips. 'We... shouldn't.'

His laugh was unsteady. 'You little liar. You want this just as much as I do.'

His hand starfished over her breast and she heard a ragged sound of pleasure as he slipped his hand inside her dress to capture the aching mound beneath. That was *her*, she realised with a shock. She who was moaning softly as if she were in pain. She who gasped as his fingertips began to rub at one sensitised nipple through her bra.

'Nikolai—' With an effort, she tried to articulate another word. 'We...'

'*Da*. We seem to make a habit of making out in cars,' he said, pushing the awry hair out of her face. 'Let me look at you.'

'But I can't look at *you*. I can't see your face properly,' she whispered, reaching up to remove the wrap-around sunglasses and then dropping them onto the dashboard. For a moment she gazed into the pale blue eyes but, blackened with lust, there was no hint of his feelings in their frozen depths.

'Is that better?' he demanded.

She nodded. 'Much better.'

'Then you are very easily pleased. Believe me, it's going to get better still, *milaya moya*.' Dipping his head, he began to kiss her again as she wound her arms around his neck like some sexy kind of cobra and he felt the slide of her tongue as it moved into his mouth and slicked against his own. It was nothing a woman hadn't done to him before but he could never remember feeling quite such an urgent shaft of lust before.

He heard her make another little moan of pleasure as he put his hand on her knee and he smiled with anticipation as she gave an impatient little wriggle of her hips. Fingers now sliding to her thighs, he felt them part for him instantly and he traced tiny circles there until she was almost incoherent with pleasure, gripping onto him as if she feared she might float away. She was ready, he thought, his heart racing with the heady anticipation of sexual release. Briefly, his fingertips tiptoed over the scorching moistness of her panties and he heard her bite back a little yelp before suddenly shattering the spell by wriggling away from him.

'Nikolai!'

Dazedly, he stared at her from between opaque eyes as she sat with her back pressed up against the car door. 'What's wrong?'

'We've got…' She sucked in a shuddering breath and then let it out again. 'We've got to stop!'

'But you don't want me to stop.'

Frantically, Zara shook her head. Of course she didn't want him to stop—or, at least, her body didn't want him to—but neither did she want him making love to her in broad daylight, either.

'Just look where we *are*,' she whispered. '*Look!* Anybody could see us.'

'But I am very dextrous, *angel moy*,' he said softly.

'And *very* discreet. I could bring you to orgasm under-neath that little dress of yours and nobody but us would know I was doing it—unless they happened to be passing at the split second when you were arching your back and moaning my name.'

His words painted a provocative image which turned her bones to water and desire warred with shock as she acknowledged his arrogant boast. 'You're…you're outra-geous,' she managed, through lips so dry they felt like sandpaper.

'I think we established that a while back, didn't we?' His eyes narrowed as he glanced down at the agitated rise and fall of her breasts. 'Stop making it difficult for yourself, Zara.' He bent his head so that he whispered his lips along the line of her jaw. 'Let's just make love.'

Her resolve at breaking point, it was his words which brought Zara back to her senses with a start. *Make love?* What the hell was he talking about? What would the instant gratification he was proposing have to do with *any* kind of emotion—least of all love? If he'd said 'let's have quick and meaningless sex' at least it would have been honest.

Distractedly, she covered her mouth with her palm and could feel her quickened breathing. She *shouldn't* have let herself get so carried away—especially after all her good intentions. And even though she could put some of the blame on Nikolai's undoubted skill—she wasn't blameless herself, was she? She had let him get intimate with her, had egged him on, like someone who was desperate for a man's touch. What if she had actu-ally capitulated? A cold sweat broke out on her fore-head. How could she actually have the courage to serve him and guests tonight if she'd actually let him…let him…?

Uncomfortably, she shrank even further away from him. 'I don't think so,' she said, giving her dress a quick tug so that it sat respectably on her knees as she glanced over at the clock on the dashboard. 'And besides, time is running out. I'm supposed to be serving cocktails on the terrace at seven—and I need to shower and change before that.'

He waited for the 'but' which never came—and to his astonishment Nikolai could see that she meant every word of it. He noted the defiant little tilt of her chin—a gesture which was as clear as daylight. She was turning him down!

'You're not serious?'

'Oh, but I am.'

He stared at her for a moment longer, as if daring her to continue—but continue she did, stubbornly and primly crossing her arms across her chest as if she were posing for a team photo! Bemused and more than a little frustrated, he jammed his shades back on and started the car with an angry click of the ignition. He put his foot down for the journey back and the loud noise of the engine killed the need for conversation. Not that he felt like saying very much to her, other than to ask whether she'd done some sort of intensive research into teasing men to a dangerous point of provocation. And he didn't say another word to her, apart from a curt goodbye when he dropped her off at the gate of his house and roared off towards the garage block with a noisy spurt of gravel.

Afterwards, he told himself that she must be playing more games with him—she *must* be. Women didn't turn him down. Nobody *ever* turned Nikolai Komarov down and certainly not more than once! There had to be a reason for it. He wondered if her sudden prim response had been motivated by a desire to gain access to his bedroom. To play at being mistress of his house, perhaps? Or simply to extract from him an even more generous pay-cheque than the one he was already offering her?

For the first time in his adult life, his ego felt bruised and, although he didn't particularly like the feeling, neither did he dwell on it. All he knew was he hadn't felt this lustful for a long time, and, inexplicably, this little waitress had fed that hunger with her reluctant behaviour. She was running rings round him and now it had become more than desire—it was a matter of pride. Did she really think that she would be able to resist him much longer when it was as clear as the blue sky above that she was hot for him, too?

Maybe some men might have cut their losses and walked away—found a lover who was far more suitable for their life and needs. But Nikolai never gave up on what he wanted and he wanted Zara Evans.

He *had* to have her.

CHAPTER SIX

IF ZARA had been in London she might have got another waitress to cover her shift that night. Anything other than having to face Nikolai again, after that sexy encounter on the mountainside. But she wasn't in London—she was trapped in the Russian oligarch's luxurious villa in the south of France with nobody to turn to. And with barely enough time to shower away the heat of the afternoon and the memory of what had so nearly happened in his sports car, before going out onto the terrace with a tray of Cosmopolitans and a smile which felt like a grimace.

Crystal had changed into a sheath of a dress covered completely with silver sequins, her newly washed hair falling in a white-gold curtain to her waist. She kept giggling wildly at everything Nikolai said, while her oblivious partner Sergei perspired gently beside her and kept checking his cell-phone.

Deliberately, Nikolai held Zara's gaze as she offered him a drink. 'You've caught the sun, Zara,' he said silkily.

'Yes.'

'Have you been sunbathing?'

For a moment the blue eyes held her captive and heat rushed to her cheeks as she saw his mouth harden into a sensual curve. Was he deliberately trying to make her feel uncomfortable by reminding her of that steamy encounter? She guessed that he would if he could. With an effort, she pushed away distracting thoughts of his fingers drifting intimately over her body. 'No, sir,' she said crisply.

'I'm very pleased to hear it. You should protect yourself at all costs.' His eyes glittered as he paused. 'It was certainly very hot out there today, wasn't it?'

'Nikolai!' chided Crystal. 'Will you stop it? She's only trying to do her job and you're making the poor girl blush!'

And even though the 'poor girl' tag rankled, in that moment Zara actually found herself warming towards Crystal for getting Nikolai off her back.

At least the meal was lavish enough to require all her concentration, since the chef had decided to present a range of delicious culinary set-pieces to impress the dinner guests. She tried to keep her eyes averted whenever she had to offer something to Nikolai, but he seemed to take great pleasure in goading her until she was forced to look at him. And then she would tremble as she read the erotic messages he was sending out from the mocking slant of his eyes. Was he deliberately leaning back in his chair to watch her as she moved around—his gaze seeming to burn into her? To remind her of just what he had been doing to her that afternoon—and the way she had responded to him so hungrily?

It was the longest evening of her life and, even though Zara couldn't wait for it to end, part of her was dreading it, too. Because what was going to happen once it was over? Was Nikolai determined to finish what had been so frustratedly halted in his sports car? And if he came to her room once the guests had gone to bed—what then? He was her boss, after all—and hadn't they already established that he could do what the hell he liked?

Zara bit her lip as she unloaded a tray in the kitchen, hating the thoughts which flooded into her mind. Because she didn't think for a moment that he would *demand* she respond to his advances—why would he need to do that when he'd witnessed her behaving like a piece of molten candle-wax whenever he touched her? But if he demanded to speak to her…could she honestly resist him?

But Nikolai did not come. He dismissed her soon after midnight—when he, Sergei and Crystal were sitting drinking calvados on the terrace—and Zara walked back to her room over the moon-washed paths, feeling inexplicably empty. As if there was a party going on to which she hadn't been invited—which was actually very true.

She showered and slipped on a little cotton nightie, climbing in between the crisp cool sheets and hoping that sleep might claim her and put an end to her tumultuous thoughts. And to her surprise, it did. She must have been more tired than she'd thought because when she awoke, it was morning.

Blinking her eyes as she opened up the shutters, she couldn't rid herself of a curious feeling of *flatness*—and, yes, of disappointment, too. How stupid women could be, she told herself crossly as she pulled on her white shirt and black skirt. *You're angry because he didn't come to you last night. Because it shows that he was merely playing with you.*

She took herself off to serve breakfast and it felt almost like being back in the sleepy little village of St Jean Gardet, because the kitchen was completely deserted. There was no sign of the chef—and no sign that he might have risen early to start the meal by chopping fruit or warming bread and croissants.

So what did she do? Had he overslept and should she go and wake him? The trouble was that she didn't have a clue where his room was.

For a moment she stood lost in thought, staring at the pristine oak table which was usually cluttered with bowls and wooden spoons and other utensils, when she heard a whistling sound from behind her and breathed a sigh of relief. Waitresses might spend their time moaning about chefs, but they certainly couldn't do without them.

'Thank goodness you're here,' she said, turning to greet him. 'I was beginning to think that you'd…' But her words tailed off into disbelieving silence when she saw that it wasn't the chef standing there. Instead, she was confronted with the sight of Nikolai—holding a freshly baked baguette in his hand and somehow managing to make even *that* look sexy.

Something unknown glittered at the depths of his ice-blue eyes and his jaw was dark with the shadow of new growth. There was an edgy and dangerous air about him this morning, she thought, with a sudden nervous skitter of her heart. And he was *still wearing the formal black suit and white silk shirt that he'd had on at dinner last night!* 'What…what on earth are you doing here?' she stumbled.

Nikolai surveyed her clear green eyes and scrubbed face, the plain black skirt and the frumpy shoes, and felt his throat thicken. 'It's my house, remember?'

'No, I mean…' Desperately, she looked over his shoulder, as if expecting to see other people walking in behind him. 'Where's the chef?'

'I gave him the day off.'

The significance of this statement confused her. 'But what about breakfast?'

He held the baguette aloft. 'What do you think this is for?'

With trembling fingers, she reached for the fruit knife. *Act normally*, she told herself fiercely. *You're adaptable, Zara—remember?* 'Okay,' she said, trying to inject a bright and breezy note into her voice. 'So I'd better start preparing the—'

But he halted her with the brief brush of his hand over hers, which made the knife slip uselessly from between her suddenly trembling fingers and clatter onto the work surface. 'I don't think I want you with a knife in your hand while I'm in the vicinity, *angel moy*,' he purred. 'Shall we think of something else for you to do instead?'

Her heart thumped. 'But your guests will be down for breakfast soon.'

'Actually, they won't.'

Now her confusion was magnified. 'They won't?'

He shook his head, put the bread down on the side and pulled off his tie. 'No, they've gone.'

She stared at the tie, which he had dropped so that it lay in a silken ebony coil on the oak table, and wondered if he had somebody to clear up after him wherever he went. 'Gone where?'

'After you went to bed last night, the three of us headed down to the casino at Monte Carlo—Sergei is fond of gambling and Crystal decided that her new dress needed a bigger audience than the one she was getting here. We played cards for most of the night and then they decided they were too tired to journey all the way back here.' He threw her a speculative glance. 'So I came back alone.'

'Stopping only to give the chef the day off and to buy bread,' she said slowly as she lifted her eyes to his. 'I don't understand.'

'Don't you?' He looked at her curiously. Was she really as innocent as she sometimes seemed? For a moment, those bright green eyes of hers looked completely guile-less. 'I was actually thinking about your sensibilities, *angel moy*,' he declared softly as the step he took closed the space between them. 'I thought you might welcome the opportunity for us to be alone together. To have the run of the house without interference—so that we can make love in private instead of all these frustrated en-counters we seem to keep having in cars.'

Zara's mouth dried. Now that he was this close, the shadow of new growth at his jaw seemed to flaunt an overt and unashamed virility, while the bright glitter from his eyes was making all her defences slowly crum-ble. Desperately, she tried to cling onto her determina-tion not to fall into a situation which would lead her to nothing but hurt and heartache. *You're nothing to him, Zara—just a part-time waitress who lied.* 'But I have no intention of letting you make love to me.'

Nikolai's mouth curved into a cynical smile. How smoothly those fabrications dropped from her lips, he told himself. How could she honestly come out with a statement like that when her eyes were just begging him to kiss her? 'Oh, really?' he questioned as he pulled her into his arms, so that her lips were mere inches away. 'Do you want to prove that to me?'

'I shouldn't…' But instead of protesting, all she could do was register the painful elevation of her heart as his mouth grazed negligently over hers.

'Shouldn't?'

'Have to…'

'Have to what?'

Closing her eyes, she struggled for coherent thought. 'P-prove anything.'

'No? Then humour me instead. Just kiss me, *angel moy.* Kiss me properly and then I'll be a happy man. Is that such an unreasonable request?'

She tried telling herself that *of course* it was unreasonable—that he had all the power in this situation and he was playing games with her. But somehow she was finding it impossible to listen to her own doubts. When his voice dipped into that sultry caress and was accompanied by the slow, circular movement of his thumb at the small of her back, Zara thought that if he'd asked her to leap over the moon it would have sounded like a reasonable request. 'Nikolai,' she breathed.

'Mmm?'

'I…' But her reply was lost because now he was kissing her and it seemed the most natural thing in the world to let him. On and on it went, deeper and deeper—like no kiss she'd ever experienced before. It felt like heaven—better than heaven. 'Oh, God,' she whispered as she came up for air.

'You like it?'

'No, I'm hating every second of it—can't you tell?'

With a low laugh, he pulled her tightly into his body, his mouth whispering against her ear.

'I've thought about you all night long,' he said unsteadily. 'I don't think I've ever lost quite so much money before. I couldn't give a stuff about the damned dice when all I was thinking about was how luscious and curved your body is.' Reaching down, he began to unbutton her white shirt until it was completely undone and he slid it away from her shoulders to encounter the satin skin beneath. He swallowed. 'It's just a pity I can't see a bit more of it. A situation which needs resolving immediately, don't you think?' Moving his hand round her back, he dealt with her bra—a deft flick of his fingers and it was soon gaping open.

'You've…you've done that before,' she said, from between lips which suddenly seemed to have swollen to about twice their normal size.

'So have you,' he declared unsteadily as she lifted her breasts up towards his mouth and he pushed her back towards the table.

But she hadn't—not like this. At least, it had never felt remotely like this—as if she were on some sensual merry-go-round that was fast gathering speed and giving her no opportunity to get off. As if she'd been given a crash course in making love and was about to give Nikolai all the benefits of her education. She could feel her bottom dipping against the wooden table and then he was pushing her down on top of it—his lips and his hands hot and hungry as they urgently roved over every available bit of bare flesh. And even though some lost little voice was trying to make itself heard—trying to get her to call a halt to this madness—Zara was in no mood to listen to it.

He yanked off her shirt and threw it to the floor. The bra quickly followed, while he captured one ripe and straining nipple in his mouth. She bucked with pleasure as he teased it with the light graze of his teeth and the warm flick of his tongue. And then he was slithering her skirt up around her thighs, impatient fingers hooking into her panties and sliding them down over her knees until they fluttered to the floor, like a white flag of surrender.

Shrugging off his jacket he returned his mouth to hers

again. 'I want you,' he growled, his fingers skating with delicate precision over her thighs.

'And…and I want you, too,' she blurted out, gasping as his hand moved upwards, briefly brushing over the soft fuzz of curls before plunging his fingers deep inside her molten heat.

'Yes, it seems you do,' he murmured appreciatively.

'Nikolai—'

'Come here,' he said urgently, his lips returning to her breasts, teasing them, sucking them—grazing them with the provocative scrape of his teeth. He concentrated on only her breasts until she was writhing impatiently beneath his lips. He'd been planning to take his mouth all the way down…over her belly, and beyond. But now he could see that might not be the smartest thing to do because her lips were circling towards his in a silent invitation he couldn't resist.

Reaching deep into the pocket of his trousers, he pulled out a small foil packet and Zara felt a moment of apprehension as she heard the rasp of a zip. She wished it could have been different—that there could have been some deep emotion which flowed between the two of them, which would have made it less about sex and more about making love. But she wasn't going to start acting coy now. Her words had been true. She *did* want him— more than she could remember wanting anything.

Swallowing down her reservations, she stared into his ice-blue eyes. Maybe what she was about to do with Nikolai was wrong—but right now it didn't feel like it. It felt anything *but* wrong. It felt like the best thing on offer in a life which had been spectacularly short on treats.

Undaunted by the size of his arousal, she watched as he rolled on the condom—and by now her fingers were gripping at his shoulders as she tried to pull him back down to her, eager to have him kiss her again. She could hear him laugh as her nails scratched against the soft silk of his shirt.

'Easy, tiger,' he purred, ripping the shirt from his body in a single movement, tiny buttons bouncing all over the kitchen floor as he gave a low laugh of pleasure. 'You are a very impatient woman.'

Zara didn't care how impatient she was, because now his magnificent torso was bare. Golden and gleaming, all bare and spare—she gave a little gulp as her fingers splayed over the frantic hammering of his heart. Oh, but he was magnificent. 'Nikolai,' she breathed.

The way she was touching him was driving him wild and yet all she was doing was to stroke at him with trembling fingers. 'Carry on doing that and I'm not going to be able to wait much longer,' he grated, unprepared for another of those sweet kisses at the curve of his jaw or a scrabbling little graze of his nipple with one of her fingernails.

'Then don't,' she whispered into his ear. 'Just do it to me.'

Nikolai expelled a ragged breath. He *couldn't* have waited a minute longer. She had already made him wait longer than any other woman. Parting her legs, he entered her with one long thrust and heard her little yelp of startled surprise as he began to move inside her.

For a moment, he stopped—his breath hot and tight in his chest as he gasped out the unthinkable. 'You're not a virgin?'

She guessed it would be crazy to tell him that right now she felt like one—as if she'd never known what sex felt like until now. She closed her eyes and concentrated on the fact that he filled her so completely so that it felt as if their bodies had been made for each other. 'No.'

'Then I am too big for you?' he questioned unsteadily—because she felt so…so *tight*—as if she'd never done it with *anyone* before.

'Actually you're p-perfect,' she answered tremblingly. 'Just perfect.'

Nikolai lost it—or, rather, in those next few minutes, he lost himself. Acting on instinct and impulse alone, he watched her with rapt fascination as he moved inside her. At the rise and fall of her breath and the rosy flowering of her breasts as she teetered closer and closer to the brink of orgasm. Cupping the silken globes of her buttocks, he drove deep inside her until she cried out his name and he wished he'd had the time to remove her skirt, so that she could have wrapped those delicious legs around his back.

As it was, he was completely turned on by her dishevelled state of abandonment as her head tipped back and she moaned something. He saw and felt the arching quiver of her release and then it was his turn. His turn to tumble down into that place of such remote sweetness—only, for once, he fell further than ever before. It was…incredible. Especially when she wrapped her arms around him so tightly and pressed her cheek against his, as if she couldn't bear to let him go.

He let out a long, ragged sigh as his heart-rate gradually began to thump back to normal, but he felt as lightheaded as a man at the end of a marathon. The adrenaline rush of all-night gambling followed by the erotic charge of ravishing his maid on the kitchen table made him come down like a stone being dropped off the edge of a cliff.

His lips buried contentedly in the warm hollow between Zara's damp breasts, Nikolai fell asleep.

CHAPTER SEVEN

'NIKOLAI. *Nikolai!*'

The breathless whisper pierced through the layers of sensuality which covered him and Nikolai resisted the call to drag him to the surface.

'Nikolai…will you please wake up?'

Nikolai swallowed to try to alleviate some of the dryness in his throat. It was Zara's voice he could hear. Zara, his maid. Zara, the woman he'd just made love to in the most erotic of circumstances. Slowly, his head turned and his eyelashes parted to see one delicious breast in glorious close-up, pressed right up against his face. 'Why?' he mumbled, unable to resist the desire to brush his lips against its warm weight. 'I might not want to wake up.'

'Because…' She wished he wouldn't do that. Or rather, she wished he would. But not now—and certainly not *here*. Not when she was feeling so vulnerable in every which way. 'Because we're both lying nearly naked on the table in the kitchen!'

'You weren't objecting to that a little while back, *angel moy*,' he murmured, the tip of his tongue tracing a light circle around one tight, puckered nipple.

Zara tried to ignore the corresponding shaft of desire which shot through her body and to wriggle away—but it wasn't easy when six foot three of powerful and muscular man was lying on top of you and when you didn't particularly want to go anywhere. This was both the best and worst of places to be, she thought helplessly. Wrapped in Nikolai's arms, with their warm flesh mingling in the aftermath of the most amazing sex and feeling as if she had just caught a glimpse of what heaven might be like.

It was just great sex, she told herself. *Stop reading happy-ever-after into it.*

Over his shoulder, she glanced around the room, her eyes alighting on rows of gleaming metal cooking instruments while her ears were alerted for any sounds. Yes, he'd said that he had given the chef the day off—but what about the other staff needed to maintain this massive property of his? The housekeeper—or the gardeners she'd seen toiling away in the flowerbeds? Had he remembered to dismiss them, too? What if one of them came wandering in, looking for a cold drink—or if Sergei and Crystal decided that they were bored with Monte Carlo and wanted a little bit more of the Komarov hospitality? A shudder ran through her as she imagined what they would find.

No. Much as she was tempted to let him have a sleep she suspected he badly needed, she was not going to risk being discovered in his arms, with her skirt hitched up around her waist and her panties lying on the floor.

But wasn't part of Zara's keenness to move more to do with the fact that she didn't quite know how to react to this man who had just made love to her? What had just happened between them was entirely outside her experience. She'd never had sex with her boss before. She'd never had sex on a kitchen table before. In fact, her experience with men was lamentably small—but she doubted whether Nikolai would ever believe that.

Not that she *needed* to prove anything to him, of course, she told herself fiercely. She just needed to extricate herself from this highly embarrassing situation.

'We can't stay here,' she said.

'No, I guess we can't.' Nikolai yawned. He felt comfortable. Sated. It seemed that the enforced wait had been worth it after all. What did they say? Something about hunger always making the best sauce… 'Let's go and lie by the pool. We can drink lemonade and lie in the shade and sleep.' His eyes glittered down at her. 'Or not sleep.'

It sounded tempting. Maybe too tempting. Wouldn't doing that make her start longing for the impossible—a world which would never be hers? Desperate to cling onto some sort of reality, Zara shook her head. 'I don't have a swimsuit.'

His eyes narrowed. 'You must have brought something with you.'

'No.'

'But surely…'

'Surely, what?' She could hear the defensive rise of her voice as she met the mocking challenge in his eyes. 'I don't make a habit of jumping into my clients' swimming pools.'

'I'm happy to hear it,' he murmured, his hand splaying possessively over one bent, bare thigh. 'But given that the client was me—didn't you imagine that something like this might happen?'

'What, that I'd end up being…being…ravished by you on the kitchen table?' She shook her head. 'It may come as a surprise to you, Nikolai, but no—it wasn't the first thing which sprang to mind. Were you so sure this was going to happen?'

He shrugged. 'The venue was always variable, but the outcome certainly wasn't.'

Indignation bubbling up inside her, she tried to wriggle out from under him, but he wouldn't let her. The arrogance of the man! 'Why, do you always seduce your waitresses?' she demanded.

'Never,' he answered simply, his mouth hovering close to hers. 'Do you always let your bosses seduce *you*?'

'Never,' she answered back, realising that she couldn't complain that he'd asked an insulting question, when she'd just done exactly the same.

The answer pleased him more than it should have done and he brushed his lips against hers in a lazy kiss. 'So we're equal.'

Equal? Was he kidding? How could she ever consider herself the equal of the billionaire oligarch? She shook her head, trying to concentrate—but it was very difficult to think straight when his thumb was stroking reflectively at the curve of her hip like that. 'I just feel as if I've gone back on my word,' she said.

'Oh?'

'Back in London, I told you that if I accepted the job, then I intended our relationship to be professional.'

'And maybe you meant it when you said it. But deep down you must have known that you were fighting against the inevitable. Just as you must know that it's pointless fighting it now, *angel moy*. When this kind of chemistry exists between two people, then it would be a—' he touched his palm to her breast and saw her fight to stop her eyelids from fluttering to close '—crime not to let it combust,' he finished thickly. 'In fact, I think it's going to combust again any minute now.'

'Nikolai...'

'Mmm?'

'What do you think you're...*doing*?'

'Why don't I give you another clue?'

'I...*oh*!'

He hadn't planned to make love to her again. Not yet. But neither had he planned the urgent stab of desire which was arrowing through him and which made the parting of her thighs as irresistible as the slow and delicious thrust with which he entered her. It should have been wild sex. Dirty sex. But when she whispered her fingertips on his face like that and planted those little kisses on his lips it felt like something he wasn't used to. It felt like tender sex.

'Zara,' he said unsteadily as he felt pleasure begin to pulse through his body.

'I'm here,' she whispered, her lips moving over the curve of his jaw and feeling his big body shudder as she traced him with kisses. She clung to him like someone who was drowning—and that was exactly what it felt like, she realised. Drowning in a pleasure which was mingled with a conflicting swirl of emotions. She wanted to burst with happiness at the way he was making her feel—and yet she had to keep telling herself that it wasn't real. None of this was real.

And when it was over she picked up her scattered clothes from the kitchen floor and began pulling them on over her warm and sated body, aware of his icy gaze raking over her as she tugged the rumpled skirt down over her bottom.

'Go and take a shower,' he instructed softly. 'And I'll have something sent over for you to wear by the pool.'

For a minute Zara thought about protesting—but only for a minute. Because wouldn't it be hypocritical if her pride made her refuse his offer? Act all outraged and pretend that nothing had happened between them—as if she didn't want to spend the rest of the day in his arms? She wanted him—and he wanted her. And unless she was planning on lying by his pool in her bra and pants, maybe she should just accept gracefully.

'Okay,' she said quietly.

On shaky legs she walked back to her room, where she showered and made herself a cup of coffee and sat drinking it while looking out at the beautiful mountains outside her window. She was still wrapped in a towel when Nikolai walked in—a scarlet bikini dangling from one hand, while in the other he held a matching embroidered silk kaftan.

Zara looked at them in confusion as he handed them over, her fingertips kneading at material which was as light as air and quite the most exquisite thing she'd ever seen. 'Where on earth did this come from?'

'I had it sent from one of the little boutiques at Villefranche-sur-mer.'

'Just like that?'

He shrugged. 'I'm not going to apologise for finding a solution to your clothing problem.'

'And are they used to sending out urgent consignments of swimwear whenever you ask them?'

'It's never happened before. But then, most women come a little better prepared than you.' His eyes narrowed as he saw her looking at him warily—and he was still so enthralled by her that he decided to tolerate her questions. But she had better learn that his patience would only go so far. 'It's not a big deal,' he said silkily. 'And certainly not worth spoiling the day for. So go and put it on.'

It was one of those defining moments. Zara knew

that. Most men wouldn't be able to procure a bikini to be delivered to their remote Mediterranean mansion within the hour. And that intimation of just how powerful he was gave her another pang of apprehension. She could tell him thanks, but no, thanks. That she'd thought about it and maybe she'd better catch the next available plane back to England. He might try to persuade her to change her mind—but not very hard, she suspected. There must be plenty more women like her waiting in line, eagerly waiting to take whatever he was prepared to offer.

Or she could accept his offer and wear the bikini— which would be tacitly agreeing to something else. To being his lover for the weekend. Pretending that they were equals and that this was a normal kind of relationship. She looked at him. He must have taken a shower as well, for his hair was damp and he had shaved away the darkness which had roughened his strong jaw. He wore a clean pair of jeans and T-shirt and for a moment he looked so gorgeous that Zara realised pretending was the only option she wanted to take.

They'd made love once, no—twice now. They could make love again—as many times as they wanted—but only if she realised that her function here had changed. She was no longer his waitress. Maybe she had been but she wasn't going to be donning an apron any time soon. That kitchen seduction meant that she had become his lover—and who knew how long that position would last? So why not embrace her new role with aplomb—and let herself enjoy what was on offer? A little uncomplicated pleasure after the pain of her godmother's long illness?

As her fingers moved to loosen the knot in the towel it occurred to her that 'uncomplicated' might be wishful thinking—but the look of expectation which had darkened his eyes made her past caring. The towel dropped to the floor and she saw his fists clench with tension as she slowly pulled on the bikini.

'It fits perfectly,' he said huskily.

She stared at him. 'How did you know my size?'

'I build tower blocks which are twenty stories high, *angel moy*,' he murmured. 'The dimensions of a woman who is five foot seven were never going to pose a problem.'

'Five foot seven and a half, actually,' she said gravely.

'You think that extra half-inch makes all the difference?'

'That's what they say.'

'Do they?' He smiled. 'I think that's a subject we could debate at leisure, don't you?'

'I'm always open to debate, Nikolai.'

'I'm very pleased to hear it—I always think that debate is an indication of a lively mind.'

'And it's my mind you're interested in, is it?'

'Not at the moment, no,' he growled. 'It's your body which seems to be commanding most of my attention.'

'Nikolai...' She felt warm, caressing fingers touching her thighs and her eyes closed.

'What?'

'I've only just...just...' She swallowed. 'I've only just put the bikini on.'

'So?' Swiftly he skimmed the teeny little bikini bottoms down and kicked them away. 'And I've decided that I want to see you naked again.'

His words reverberated round in her head. *I want*, he said. And Nikolai got what Nikolai wanted. Zara thrilled to the dark promise in his tone and her newly awakened body quivered in anticipation of his touch. But as he carried her towards the bed she felt a sudden sense of foreboding, too.

Because he did exactly as he pleased. He snapped his fingers and people came running. Staff came and went at his behest. He was the ringmaster who ran the whole show.

And right now—even as his lips were coming down to kiss her and transport her back to pleasure-land—she felt like one of Nikolai Komarov's obedient puppets.

CHAPTER EIGHT

'You've been remarkably quiet, *angel moy.*'

Behind the protective shield of her sunglasses, Zara studied the powerful body of her Russian lover, which gleamed like a golden statue beneath the Mediterranean sun. They were sprawled on loungers beside the vast turquoise glitter of an infinity pool, where they'd spent the day drifting in and out of sleep.

Occasionally, they'd sipped at iced drinks which Nikolai had carried from the well-stocked fridge in the pool-house—in what seemed like a neat little bit of role-reversal. In air scented by roses and jasmine, they'd eaten the bread he'd brought back that morning—spread thickly with home-made fig jam—the most delicious meal she could ever remember eating. And if she had to keep reminding herself that she wasn't dreaming, then who could blame her when this bore not even a passing resemblance to her real life?

'Mmm?' he prompted as he turned onto his side to look at her—at the shiny caramel-coloured hair, which was loose and spilling down all over the bright red tri-angles of her bikini top. Most women you couldn't shut up once you'd made love to them. But not Zara. She'd said very little which wasn't a breathless variation on his name. And, ironically, it made him curious about her in a way he was rarely curious about a lover. 'So why the sudden silence?'

Zara tried to concentrate on what he was saying to her, but it wasn't easy when he was within touching reach and wearing nothing but a pair of sleek swim-shorts. Of course she hadn't said much—she had been too dazed by what had been happening to her, and forcing herself not to question where it was all heading. And they had none of the equipment necessary for small talk, she realised. No mutual friends or acquaintances. They didn't even have the shared experience of being the same nationality. In fact, when it boiled down to it, they had absolutely nothing in common except for this urgent sexual hunger which seemed to have taken both of them by surprise.

She shrugged. 'Well, you've taken about five phone calls since we've been out here—and when you haven't been doing that, you've—'

'Been having wild and amazing sex with you?' he finished silkily, enjoying the corresponding rush of colour which flooded into her face.

She laid a cool palm over her warm cheek. 'You just struck me as the kind of man who wouldn't be particularly interested in chit-chat,' she added truthfully.

A smile curved the edges of his lips. 'How very perceptive of you,' he murmured. 'Or maybe you're much cleverer than I thought. Perhaps you've learnt the power of withholding information.'

'You make it sound like some sort of secret war,' she observed, with a sudden beat of misgiving.

'Don't they call it the battle of the sexes?'

She brushed an insect away from her arm. 'That's a little too complex for me, Nikolai. Deep down, I'm a simple soul.'

Intrigued now, he shifted his body slightly, so that

the curve of her hips and breasts were fully in his line of vision. 'And apart from being a simple soul—what else are you, Zara? How come a woman like you ends up being a waitress?'

She watched the little ladybird spread its shiny, spotty wings and fly away before she looked up at him. 'That's a pretty insulting question to ask. There's nothing wrong with being a waitress, you know.'

'I'm not saying there is. You just struck me as some-one capable of a job that's a little more imaginative. Don't you ever aspire to something other than offer-ing plates of food to people whose palates are already jaded?'

Zara smiled—because in a way his deprecating com-ment was cleverly directed at himself. He was a man whose own palate was jaded, she recognised—and that might be one of the reasons she was here with him. Was she his 'bit of rough', she wondered—someone different enough from his usual partners to awaken a bored ap-petite? 'Of course I want to do something else with my life,' she said. 'But it's not always as easy as that, and I don't ever want to knock waitressing. It's a fantastic job—it's flexible and it's varied.'

Folding his arms behind him, he pillowed his head on them and surveyed her from between narrowed eyes. 'And that's what you've always done?'

'Not always, no. In a previous existence, I was an agricultural student,' she said.

He raised his eyebrows. 'Unusual choice,' he com-mented. 'Any particular reason?'

'Oh, the usual one. I just fell in love with the land.' She shrugged her shoulders. 'I grew up in the city and that's all I ever really knew—and then one day we went on a school trip to a farm. There were only cows and sheep and a rather mangy old goat, but I was hooked. And that's when I realised that grass and mud held a certain kind of appeal. I worked hard at school and got all my grades and was accepted at college.'

'So what happened to make you jettison something you loved?'

She slid her shades up onto her head and looked at him. 'You're assuming something happened?'

'Keen students don't drop out unless they're forced to.'

'You're right, of course. They don't.' There was a pause. 'My godmother became sick—and I took some time out to care for her.'

'How very admirable,' he observed.

'I didn't do it to be admirable,' she said sharply—because wasn't there a wry undertone to his remark, as if she were making up some kind of sob story in order to tug at his heartstrings? Did people *do* that as well? she wondered suddenly. Try to engage his sympathy and hope that he'd put a big wodge of money their way?

She swallowed. 'She'd never married nor had children of her own and she put her own life on hold to bring me up when my parents were killed. I loved her, and I owed her—big time. Only, after she'd died…' Her words tailed off as a wave of sadness hit her.

His eyes narrowed as he saw her face crumple. 'What?' he asked softly.

Zara shifted slightly on the sun-lounger. 'I seemed to have been away from college for so long, and to have seen so much of a different side of life, that I wasn't sure whether I could go back and start all over again. Waitressing was something I could do without any qualifications while I gave myself time to think about my future. That's what happened.'

But Nikolai still felt as if she was leaving gaps in her account. What did they call it? Being economical with the truth. What wasn't she telling him, and why? 'And what will you do when you go back—do you have other jobs like this lined up?'

It was the best question he could have asked, because it reminded her of the great gulf which divided them. Two people from two different worlds. All that had happened was that those two worlds had briefly collided and after the weekend the universe would settle back into its normal order. *So hold onto your dignity,* she told herself fiercely. *You may have barely a penny to your name— but he will never,* ever *take pity on you.*

Hiding her fears behind a composed smile, she paused as if to give his question proper consideration. 'I haven't really decided what I'm going to do,' she said blithely. 'I'm waiting for inspiration.'

He saw the proud tilt to her chin and something stirred in his conscience. Had he misjudged her? Been too quick to spring to the conclusion that she was one of those women who wanted to get her hands on his money? She certainly hadn't been acting that way since she'd been here. There had been none of that narrow-eyed assessment as she'd surveyed the priceless artefacts in his house. In fact, she'd been more interested in the flowers in his garden. And if she was a gold-digger, then she didn't play by the traditional rules—because she certainly didn't dress like one. He thought of the simple little sundress which had still managed to look like a million dollars. The cheap little sandals which showcased her wonderful legs. He thought about how hard she'd worked at lunch and dinner—carrying heavy trays in the warm Mediterranean air, while resolutely refusing to meet his gaze and flirt. Maybe he *had* misjudged her.

'Well, if it's inspiration you're after, then maybe I can help with that.' He rose from his sun-lounger, momentarily blocking out the sun with his statuesque form—all tight, hard muscle and gleaming golden flesh. 'Ever swum naked before?'

She shook her head as she looked up at him. 'Never.'

He took off his swim shorts, then bending over her, he smiled, wondering why her lack of sexual experience should please him so intensely. 'Good,' he murmured. 'Then prepare to be inspired.'

He helped her off the sun-bed, then quickly divested her of her bikini top while she shimmed out of her bottoms. He lifted her up and slid her into water which felt like cool silk on her naked limbs. Zara could never recall feeling quite so weightless, or free before—and she kicked away from him instantly. She was a good swimmer and swam almost a length under water, emerging to blink away the shining droplets of water to find Nikolai leaning at the far end of the pool, watching her.

'You swim like a mermaid,' he said.

She laughed. 'I seem to be missing a tail.'

He caught her by the waist as she passed, brushing his lips over her wet face. 'I prefer legs,' he said softly as he found the centre of her feminine warmth, erotically contrasted with the cool lick of the water. He moved a finger with light precision. 'Don't you?'

'Without…question. Oh, Nikolai…'

His kisses were hot and hungry, his fingers practised and swift. The world became composed of nothing but intense sensation—and he brought her to orgasm so rapidly that Zara slumped helplessly against his shoulder, her eyes closed and her breath shuddering from her lips.

'You liked that,' he murmured eventually as her breathing slowed against his skin.

'Mmm.' Fractionally, she moved away from him—reaching down to capture the hard heat between his legs, her hand closing over his velvety shaft. 'And do you like this?'

'Yes, I like it,' he ground out urgently as she slid her fingers over him with insistent, silky movements—until he, too, groaned his own release.

For a while they stayed locked in each other's arms as the water lapped against them and then he lifted her from the water and carried her out to one of the loungers, where he wrapped her in a vast and fluffy towel.

He watched as her eyes drifted to a close and it occurred to him that maybe he could have offered her some more imaginative inspiration than mere sex. Couldn't he have suggested a few of his wealthy colleagues who might be looking for permanent waiting staff—would that have helped? Maybe that was something he should bear in mind.

She was sleeping now, so he went and sat out of earshot and made a few more calls. And later, he took her out to dinner—after first reassuring her that the dress she'd brought from England was fine.

'Honestly?'

'Honestly,' he said quietly. 'The way your skin is glowing and your hair is shining—I think you could probably get away with wearing sackcloth.'

'That's not the most reassuring answer you could have given me, Nikolai,' she said gravely, and he laughed.

Through the darkening mountains, they drove to St Jean Gardet—where the village had sprung to life. Zara looked around as the powerful car bumped to a halt in the main square, finding it hard to imagine that this was the same sleepy place she'd stumbled upon yesterday. Shops were open and people were strolling around in holiday mood. Lights gleamed from trees and restaurant tables spilled out onto the cobbled stones, so that laughter and chatter carried on the still night air.

Beneath the stars, they ate steak-*frites* and drank red wine and Zara wished she could have hung onto that moment for ever. *Is this what it feels like when you start to fall in love?* she wondered as she stared across the table at Nikolai's angled face. *As if everything is perfect and exactly as it should be. As if you have everything you ever wanted, right there at your fingertips.*

'It's so gorgeous here,' she said, looking around and trying to fix the moment in her mind. 'And the woman who was so surly to me in the *tabac* has just said *"bon appétit"*.'

'That's because you're with me.'

She bit back a smile. 'I'd sort of worked that one out for myself.'

He thought how huge her eyes looked tonight and how dark and kiss-bruised her lips. She had piled her hair up high on her head so that only a few loose tendrils were dangling down around her face—and it occurred to him that by now he should be growing a little bit bored. Too much unbroken time in one woman's company was usually enough to make him want to make his excuses, and leave.

Usually.

He leaned back in his chair and studied her. Was it her lack of sophistication which was responsible for the unfamiliar sense of ease he was experiencing in her company? Or because he had known from the outset that there could be no future in it? *And there is no future in it*, he reminded himself as his pager went off in his pocket.

He took the call with the news that the New York

merger was finally going ahead—and in a way it made his decision for him. He would have to bring his schedule forward and cut short this weekend. He saw Zara's tentative little smile at him over the rim of her glass and thought that maybe it was for the best—because he suspected she was starting to care for him, and that was certainly not what he had intended.

She was no virgin. In fact, she was one of the most exciting and inventive lovers he had ever known—and yet in a funny sort of way she seemed terribly innocent. She was also very sweet and he didn't want her to get hurt. And didn't he always hurt women—no matter how unintentionally—because he could never give them what they wanted?

'Did I mention that I have to go to New York tomorrow?' he questioned suddenly. 'Which means that I'll have to fly out first thing.'

Painfully, Zara's heart slammed beneath her breast and the previous peace of the evening disintegrated. So this was it. The goodbye she had been expecting—only not quite so soon, nor quite so brutally executed. And she was going to have to take it on the chin.

'No, no, you didn't mention it.' In the candlelight, she forced a bright smile. 'But I was supposed to be leaving tomorrow anyway and I guess I *am* a little redundant—now that your guests have gone.'

For some reason he felt bad. 'Perhaps we can meet up in London some time?' he suggested.

But Zara was certain she heard evasion in his voice and she forced herself to heed it. Because she knew that their paths would never cross in London—not unless she happened to be working, and how awkward would it be if she tried to follow it up? To try to make their brief fling into something it wasn't—and destroy her good memories of it in the process. This place had been like an oasis, she thought. She should look on it as a beautiful interlude after a tough year and put it down to experience.

'Perhaps,' she answered politely.

'Shall I get the bill?'

Zara nodded and picked up her handbag. 'Yes, please.'

He drove back to the villa and took her to his bedroom—a place of restrained and very masculine luxury—where he proceeded to make love to her. But even as her body splintered with pleasure as he wrapped her in his powerful arms Zara felt curiously distanced by the whole experience. As if some self-protective instinct were already encasing her emotions in ice—to stop her from getting hurt.

In the morning, she awoke to find him getting dressed and she watched from between slitted eyes as he pulled on a silk shirt and tucked it into his dark, tapered trousers. She thought how shuttered his features appeared—as if he was lost in thought and had already moved on.

'You're awake,' he said softly.

She blinked in surprise. 'You noticed.'

Walking over to the bed, he saw the tumble of her hair spread over his pillows and the rise and fall of her luscious breasts. 'I notice everything about you. I noticed the way your breathing changed and the way your body stirred. And I'd much rather be *here*,' he said thickly, his hand moving down over the sheet to rest in the fork between her thighs, 'than on a damned plane.' He leaned over to plant a lingering kiss on her lips. 'A car will come and collect you later and take you to the airport. In the meantime help yourself to anything you want. Have a swim. Use the hot tub. I want you to enjoy your last few hours here. And safe journey home, Zara.'

Quickly, she sat up, the sheet falling to her waist as she heard what essentially amounted to a dismissal. The party was over—and it was time to get back to being who she really was. 'And you.'

He went over to the bureau, where he picked up a long white envelope, which he waggled at her. 'Oh, and by the way—your cheque is here.'

She blinked. 'M-my cheque?'

'Your wages.' He raised his eyebrows. 'Remember? The reason you came here? Big money.'

'Of course.' *Big money? The reason you came here?* Zara only just stopped herself flinching at his crass references and the sudden mention of money in the bedroom made her want to curl up and die. Awkwardly, she grabbed at the sheet and held it up against her chin.

'Don't cover yourself up,' he said softly.

'I feel naked.'

'That's because you are naked and someone with a body like yours should never sully it with clothes.' For a moment he just stared at her long and hard—as if committing her to memory—before glittering her a last, brief smile. 'Goodbye, *angel moy.*'

'Goodbye, Nikolai.'

The words tore at her as she waited until she heard the sound of his car leaving, then she slipped over to the window to see his silver sports car snaking its way over the mountain road towards the airport. Her heart was hammering furiously and some dread feeling at the pit of her stomach made her go to the bureau and pick up the envelope, her fingers trembling as she pulled out the cheque which lay inside.

She stared down at it in disbelief. It was not the amount they had agreed on back in London—it was more than double that, and a huge payment for the meagre amount of work she'd done, by anyone's estimation.

Zara felt physically sick. Why had he done this? Made such an expansive gesture after what had happened. Had he actually *paid her for the sex*? Was that what this ridiculous sum was all about?

For a moment she had to sit down until she had recovered herself, telling herself that now was not the time to go to pieces. Her mind raced with possibilities about how she should react, but she knew that only one thing would give her any degree of satisfaction—no matter how foolish it might be in the long run. Her hands were still shaking as she ripped the cheque into tiny shreds, threw them into one of the bureau drawers before closing it shut with a bang. A cleaner wouldn't dare touch anything in his drawers, she thought grimly—so let *him* find it.

Running down to her staff accommodation at the back of the vast estate, she threw her clothes into the small case—not caring that she was crumpling and creasing them in the process. And then with hot tears spilling down her cheeks she sat huddled on the bed, looking out at the misty Provençal mountains as she waited for the car to take her to the airport.

CHAPTER NINE

FOR the third time in a row, the phone went dead in his ear and Nikolai stared at it with a growing feeling of disbelief. Had she hung up on him—*again*? He shook his head. No. It was inconceivable. How could the sexy little waitress who should have been grateful for all he'd given her have possibly slammed the phone down on him?

He paced the floor of his penthouse office which gave a picture postcard view of London—and which he had once vowed never to take for granted—but for once the soaring skyline made no impression on him. *What the hell was she playing at?*

He clicked his intercom and one of his aides came on the line immediately. 'That woman, Zara Evans?' he said crisply. 'You remember—the one I asked you to find for me?'

'*Da*, Nikolai.'

'Do we have an address for her?'

'Of course.'

'Then send someone round there. Now. I want to know when she's there and I want to know who she's with.'

His fury growing as the minutes ticked away, he had to wait until past midnight before word came through that she'd arrived home—alone—presumably after she'd finished one of her shifts. Nikolai knew it would be sensible to leave what he had to say until the next morning—the trouble was that he wasn't feeling in a particularly sensible mood. He was feeling impatient, angry and mystified—and none of this was helped by remembering the way she'd kissed him when he had been deep inside her body...

At half-past midnight his limousine came to a halt in front of a tiny mid-terrace house in a run-down part of town he was unfamiliar with. Dustbins stood at the front of each property—presumably because there was nowhere else to store them—and further down the road graffiti had been scrawled on a wall. It was the kind of place where shops were boarded up after dark—or where a car might find its tyres missing in the morning.

The driver turned round with a frown on his face. 'You sure this is the right place, boss?' he questioned, in Russian.

For a moment, Nikolai was quiet. It certainly wasn't the worst place he'd seen in his life—far from it—and every city in the world had areas where the less fortunate lived. But these days he rarely encountered poverty and it took him back to a time and place which he usually kept locked away. Funny how vividly it all came back, if he let it. Memories vivid enough to make the little hairs on the back of his neck stand on end now came into sharp focus. A Moscow tenement, an apartment shared with three other families. The cold eyes and suspicious glances of his hungry neighbours. And a boy who did whatever he could to get a ruble to put food in his mouth.

His mouth hardened as he got out of the car and rang the bell on a fading door. It took a moment or two before a hall light went on and she must have peered out through the spy-hole because he heard her voice and the note of disbelief in it.

'Nikolai? Is that you?'

'Expecting someone else?'

'What…what are you doing here?'

'I want to talk to you.'

'Well, I don't…' From behind the protection of the closed door, Zara sucked in a deep breath and willed him to go away. *But you don't want him to go away, do you? Not really. Haven't you been lying sleepless, night after night—just remembering the way he kissed you? And regretting an impetuous gesture that you could ill afford to make.* 'I don't want to talk to you,' she finished. 'And it's late.'

'I know it's late—and if you don't open the damned door then I'll keep knocking until all your neighbours wake up.'

'You can't do that.' But she knew that he could—and probably would—so she loosened the chain and opened the door, to see him standing like some unmoveable force on her door step. 'That's blackmail,' she accused.

'Net,' he negated grimly as he saw her tug the lapels of her cheap cotton dressing gown closer together. 'It is known as getting what you want.'

'Which we both know you always do.'

If only she knew, he thought grimly. If only she knew. 'Oh, always,' he agreed mockingly as he stepped inside and looked around the cramped hallway. 'You look as if you've fallen on hard times,' he observed slowly. 'Or does it always look like this?'

Zara flushed. 'I've lived here since I was a little girl,' she defended. 'And it may not be looking at its best at the moment, but I haven't really had the chance to do much decorating lately.'

'But this street…' His words tailed off and he looked into the defiant green gaze of her eyes.

A fierce sense of pride made her want to explain—though part of her wondered whether someone like Nikolai would have any comprehension of what she was talking about. 'When I was growing up—it was different. Families lived in this area and people took pride in their houses then. Now most of them are rented out. I'm hoping to put it on the market soon—and, while it may not be a multimillion dollar villa in the south of France, it's clean,' she added proudly. 'And it's home.'

His eyes narrowed. 'And presumably you survive on just your waitressing salary—which is not a particularly high salary?'

'That's right.'

He stared at her. 'So how come you dramatically ripped up the cheque I left you?'

Incredulously, she stared back. 'You know exactly why.'

'If I knew, then I wouldn't be asking.'

'Think about it!' she bit out as she turned on her heel and walked into the sitting room, hearing his footsteps following behind her. And suddenly, she was terribly afraid that she would go to pieces. Say or do something she might later regret—because the truth was that she hadn't been able to get him out of her mind, or her heart. She'd barely had a single thought that didn't involve her Russian lover. *Ex*-lover, she reminded herself fiercely.

Reaching down into a cupboard, she found a dusty bottle of livid-coloured orange liqueur, which had been there for as long as she could remember, and poured a measure into a little glass. 'Do you want any?' she asked ungraciously.

'Tempting. But I think I'll pass.'

Zara sipped at the fiery spirit, grateful for the instant little boost of energy it gave her. Drinking at midnight wasn't a pastime she indulged in regularly, but it had been a long day. There had been a big directors' lunch, followed by afternoon tea, and then she'd grabbed at an extra job which had come in, only to discover that it had been a windswept party on a river-boat which had been full of drunken stockbrokers who kept being sick over the side.

'So, why?' he persisted.

She turned round, trying to buffer herself against the impact he made on her, but it wasn't easy—especially since all his undeniable attributes seemed amplified when measured against the humble background of her tiny sitting room. He was wearing a dark suit and crisp white shirt, and his only concession to relaxation had been to loosen his tie.

'You paid me over double what I was owed!' she accused.

He raised his eyebrows. 'That's the first time some-one's ever complained that I've *over*paid them,' he drawled.

'Don't be obtuse, Nikolai—you know exactly what I mean.'

'No, I don't. I thought you were good at your job and deserved the extra payment.'

'What, for the *extra services provided*?'

He froze. 'You think I was paying you for sex?'

'What else was I supposed to think?'

'You think that I'm the kind of man who *pays for sex*?'

'Can we keep your ego out of it for a moment? This isn't about *you*, it's about *me*,' she shot back, swallowing down the intense hurt she still felt at the memory of him waving that wretched envelope at her as if she were some kind of hooker. 'So why the over-generous gesture, if not for that?'

For a moment he was silent as he battled with his feelings, angry that she was forcing him to offer some kind of explanation—he who never had to explain himself to anyone. But the confusion and the undoubted hurt in her brilliant green eyes made him change the habit of a lifetime. 'I realised that I'd misjudged you,' he said heavily. 'That you were not the woman I thought you to be.'

Zara stared at him warily. 'And what kind of woman was that?'

'They're known in the business as gold-diggers,' he said acerbically, and saw her wince.

'How very flattering,' she said quietly.

'Oh, you may think it's nothing but a misogynistic tag but believe me, I've met plenty of them in my time.' His mouth hardened. 'Which might explain why I'm more than a little suspicious of the opposite sex—most of whom seem to want something from me. Perhaps the money was a compensation for my own sense of guilt when I realised you were nothing like that. And I often tip my staff,' he added. 'The sex had absolutely nothing to do with your pay-cheque.'

Zara put down the sticky little glass of liqueur and shrugged. 'I guess I'm partly to blame. It's my own fault. I should have just done the job I was supposed to be there for and then I could have walked away with a clear conscience and none of this misunderstanding would have ever happened. I shouldn't have...'

'Shouldn't have, what?' he prompted softly.

'Shouldn't have *let you*.' She swallowed down the poignant and bittersweet memories of their love-making.

'I shouldn't have let myself. It was a stupid, stupid thing to do.'

Something in her soft contrition hit him like a slow-motion fist to the solar plexus and Nikolai felt a sharp pang of remorse. 'But you couldn't help yourself,' he said simply. 'And neither could I. The chemistry between us was so powerful—too powerful to stop. Maybe impossible. Or do you think that kind of reaction between two people happens all the time?'

'I don't know.'

'You haven't had many lovers?'

She stared down at a bare patch in the faded carpet. Why pretend to be something she wasn't? He knew she'd never swum nude until she'd done it with him and he knew several other things she hadn't tried before he had taught her how to do them in graphic and glorious detail...

'No. Actually, I've had precisely one before you.'

Dark brows knitted together. *'One?'*

'Is that so bizarre?'

'It's unusual for a woman of your age. At least, it is among the kind of women I usually associate with.' It seemed to indicate that sex was a big deal for her—something which should have made him turn his back on her and run as fast as his legs could take him. And yet he could feel a sudden warm satisfaction suffusing his veins, the slow smile which curved his lips with pleasure. 'And was he a good lover?' he questioned. 'The man you thought you might marry, perhaps?'

'Actually, he was neither. Just somebody I was at college with who was more into rugby and beer than giving a woman pleasure.' She gave a short laugh. 'Until he found a farmer's daughter with several thousand acres to her name. It just took him a while to get around to telling me—and it seemed that everyone else at college knew before I did.'

He mulled over what she had just told him. A man who was not committed to giving a woman pleasure implied that she had not known real pleasure before. Could that explain those little choking tears he'd seen her try to bite back when he had made her come, over and over again?

For the first time since he had stormed in there, he looked at her properly, and that in itself was odd, because a woman's body was usually the first thing he looked at.

She must have just got ready for bed because her face was scrubbed and a single plait hung down over her cotton dressing gown. It was a commonplace piece of attire—the light material was sprigged with flowers and her legs and feet were bare. She was pretty, yes—and her body was quite delicious. But there were a million women more stunning than Zara Evans. So how come he wanted to bend her into his arms every time he saw her?

'Zara,' he said softly.

The note in his voice made her flesh turn to goose-bumps but she continued to stare at the bare patch on the carpet as if her life depended on it. 'Don't,' she whispered.

'Don't what?'

'You know very well what,' she said, a note of desperation touching her voice.

'Look at me.'

Zara shook her head. If she looked at him she would be lost—she would drown in the depths of his pale blue eyes and start longing for things which could never be hers.

'Zara?'

And then she found she couldn't resist—not a moment longer. Her gaze was drawn upwards to his face, where hunger curved his sensual lips and ice-fire blazed sexual promise from his eyes.

'Don't do this,' she whispered.

'I can't help myself—and neither can you.'

He reached out then and pulled her into his arms and she went, unresisting—eager for passion and comfort. And hadn't it felt like a lifetime since she had run her fingers through the tumble of his hair? Or pressed herself into the hard sinews of his body and raised her face eagerly to his? She could hear the deepening unsteadiness of his breath as he kissed her and the tension in his powerful body which communicated itself to her. His hands were on her breasts now, splaying possessively over their aching weight, and he made a tiny groan as his fingers encountered the rock-hard tips.

'I've been thinking about you every damned night,' he ground out as he tore his mouth away from hers. 'About doing this. Touching *this*.' He felt her wild tremble. 'Have you thought about me, too, Zara?'

'Yes! *Yes!*'

'Then come home with me,' he demanded hotly. 'Come home with me now.'

The urgency in his voice took her by surprise and the practised caress of his fingers was setting her blood on fire. But even though it nearly broke her to do so, Zara shook her head, because she could see the danger in what he was suggesting. If she wasn't careful, he would swallow her up and spit her out—leaving her with nothing but a broken heart. She had to hang onto her independence if she was going to survive. She *had* to. 'I c-can't,' she said breathlessly as she felt him begin to ruck the nightdress

up over her thighs. 'At least, not tonight. It's too late. I…
have to get up very early in the morning and all my stuff
is here.'

'You don't have to do anything you don't want to.'

'Yes, I *do*, Nikolai. I work for a living, remember?
And I *need* to work.'

He heard the note of determination in her voice and a
wave of incredulity washed over him as he realised that
she actually meant it. He wanted to tell her not to be so
ridiculous and that he would recompense her for any lost
wages. Yet he suddenly realised that he couldn't have it
both ways. He could hardly complain about women bleed-
ing men dry of money if he wasn't prepared to applaud
someone who did the exact opposite.

'Well, if you need to work, then you can't allow senti-
ment to cloud your judgement,' he said, his voice heavy
with frustration. 'You will accept the money that I owe
you for the south of France job—and then we won't
speak of it again. Is that understood?'

She nodded, lifting her throat so that he could run
his mouth over it—revelling in the warm brush of his
breath and the fact that now she didn't have to bear the
consequences of her rash action. 'Yes.'

'And tomorrow, you will pack a bag—with everything
you need—and you will spend the night at my house.
Okay?'

'Okay.' His fingers were brushing negligently over the
warm fuzz at the juncture of her thighs and she squirmed
impatiently beneath them. 'And n-now…?'

'Now?' He dipped his hand, pleased that she was
naked beneath the little nightdress, his fingers delv-
ing into her moist heat as she bucked with pleasure.
One more night, he told himself—a week at most—and
then he would be free of her. He could feel her hunger,

could detect the evocative scent of sexual desire which throbbed in the air around them, and felt himself harden even more. Nikolai swallowed. He could take her here. It would be so easy. On that rather beaten-up old sofa over there—or even up against the wall. With aching clarity, he could imagine her thighs wrapped fervently around his back as he drove into her long and deep and brought them both to orgasm. He could carry her upstairs and share what would doubtless be a cramped bed—but who cared about that when two people felt like this?

Or he could make her wait—as she had made *him* wait! The tip of his tongue edged over his dry lips. It would be a lesson to her—and to him. Show her that she wasn't the only one who could hold out. Remind him that, yes, he was hot for her—very hot—but he didn't let women walk all over him. Certainly not more than once. He was the boss and she had better accept that fact and start fitting in with *his* plans.

His fingers stilled and he moved his hand away from her slick heat to the accompaniment of the slump of her body against him and a whispered little moan of disappointment.

'Now you need your sleep, I think,' he said pleasantly. He tugged her nightdress back down and saw her lips shiver with disappointment—but he steeled his heart against their appeal. 'And so do I.' His kiss was perfunctory because he didn't trust himself to stay there a moment longer and his voice was cool and matter-of-fact. 'Phone my secretary tomorrow and she will arrange for a car to collect you.'

CHAPTER TEN

IT WAS only supposed to be one night.

One night to rid himself of her hypnotic spell—that was all. But one night somehow became two and two became three. Before Nikolai fully appreciated what was happening, Zara seemed to be firmly ensconced in his Kensington home. She was the face he awoke to each morning. The person he found himself eager to see at the end of a working day. The reason he refused every one of the swathe of invitations which regularly dropped through his letter box—for why would he want to make small talk with high-flyers when he could be at home in bed with his green-eyed beauty? One who had stubbornly insisted on continuing with her waitressing, despite all his enticements for her to be at his beck and call whenever he wanted her. And he hadn't been able to change her mind, no matter what tactics he employed. Why, he didn't think he'd ever met a woman as stubborn or as independent as Zara Evans!

Was that all part of her appeal, he mused, that determination not to let him call all the shots? The recognition that here was a woman who worked just as hard as he did—albeit in a much more modest field. And once the novelty value of all that had faded, then surely this *hunger* for her would have burnt itself out—and he could get back to living normally. Alone.

It was just that he seemed to have forgotten how to do normal. Here he was, standing shaving, his mind completely preoccupied—while through the open door leading to his bedroom lay the source of his preoccupation, her hair all tousled and a lazy smile of satisfaction curving her lips into an upward tilt.

Was she aware that she was weaving some strange kind of spell over him? he wondered savagely. And wasn't it time he tried to break free from it?

'You look miles away,' he commented as he walked back into the bedroom.

His deeply accented voice cut into her thoughts and Zara looked up, her stomach dissolving with familiar lust as she watched him. He was wearing nothing but a white towel knotted at the hips, while he rubbed a smaller version through the damp tumble of his dark gold hair. Droplets of water gleamed like precious metal on his bare torso and she swallowed down a feeling of disbelief. That *she* should be here, in Nikolai's bed. And that he should be looking back at her with that familiar spark of hunger in his ice-blue eyes.

She sighed. The bed was nearly as big as her entire bedroom back home and her body felt all warm. She ached, yes—but it was a luscious kind of ache, which reminded her of all the things her Russian lover had done to her in the long night which had passed. And all the nights before that…

'How can I be miles away when I'm right here?' she questioned, with a shy smile.

With a ragged sigh, Nikolai dropped the towel, hearing her stifled little gasp as he treated her to a back view of his naked body. He felt the answering pull of arousal and knew that if he turned around and walked over to the bed he could be inside her eager body within seconds. And that he wanted to be. He wanted to get on the phone to his secretary and tell her to cancel all his meetings for the rest of the day just so he could stay home with Zara. Savagely, he pulled a silk shirt from his wardrobe.

Because hadn't he expected her allure to have faded a little by now? It had been over a month since they had returned from France—and three weeks since she had first shared his bed in England. Usually, he rationed out his time and women were grateful for whatever they got. A couple of nights here and there, depending on how the mood took him. Some nights he preferred to work late and to sleep alone. Or he liked the freedom to go and play cards until dawn. Or to fly to the other side of the world with only his closest staff knowing his exact whereabouts.

But with Zara it was as if he had thrown the rule-book out of the window. It was as if he couldn't get enough of her and he couldn't for the life of him work out why. As if her tender kisses and amazing body had sparked off some kind of powerful addiction, which kept needing to be fed.

Why, just the other night he'd woken up and lain staring at the ceiling, with her all snuggled up beside him, her silken hair spread over his chest. He'd tried to move and she had made a gurgling little murmur of protest in his ear—and he hadn't wanted to wake her because he'd known she had an early shift in the morning. *He hadn't wanted to wake her because she had a shift in the morning!* So he'd stayed in an uncomfortable position until she'd rolled away of her own accord. Leaving him wondering whether he was losing his mind as well as his independence.

Was she aware that somehow she'd lured him into her little honey trap and was she building up little fantasies about the future even now, while fixing him with that dreamy smile? Was she perhaps thinking that the sexual compatibility they shared might overlap in a more general way? Nikolai's face hardened. Some women didn't need very much to let their minds wander down the white lace and diamond route—especially when a man had never been married before and had been tagged with that tiresome 'eligible' label. And if Zara was doing that—could he really blame her? Wasn't it time that she got some sense of what he was really like—the kind of man he really was? To warn her that any kind of long-term wish fulfilment was a waste of her time?

'You're not working tonight, are you?' he questioned idly.

Zara swallowed as he began to pull on a pair of silk boxers. Sometimes when she watched him getting dressed it seemed even more intimate than when they'd actually been having sex. It *was* intimate, she realised. Why, when she'd seen Emma at the book-launch party yesterday lunchtime, her friend had exclaimed that she and Nikolai were practically *living* together. And when Zara had protested—rather feebly, it was true—Emma had said something on the lines of did-she-realise-what-kind-of-man-she-was-dealing-with? That a man who was known as a commitment-phobe was not the kind of person you should lose your heart to.

And Zara had shrugged and said that there was no way she was losing her heart to him—and she certainly wasn't stupid enough to imagine that she and Nikolai might have some kind of long-term future together.

Except that wasn't entirely true, was it? Even when common sense told you one thing, that didn't seem to

stop your heart from longing for the complete opposite... Hadn't she seen him lying asleep beside her one
morning, his dark lashes feathering into two arcs above
his high, carved cheekbones—and hadn't she started to
wonder what his son or his daughter might look like?
His daughter would be very beautiful, she mused—if
she inherited those ice-blue eyes and dark gold hair.

Coming out of an engrossing daydream about little
Svetlana Komarov's first birthday party, she realised that
Nikolai was standing there, half naked and waiting for
an answer to his question, and for a minute she blushed.
Imagine if he'd been able to read her mind!

'No, I'm not working tonight. I...well, you know I requested daytime shifts wherever possible? And Emma's
mum is still absolutely fine about it, so I've got most
evenings off.'

'Good.' He glimmered her a cool smile as he began
to button up his shirt. Of course he was *pleased* that he
could have the evenings with her. He hated seeing her
going off each day to wait on men who were doubtless
eyeing the luscious swell of her breasts instead of what
was on the tray she was offering them. But maybe it was
time they started venturing out beyond the bedroom.
Stop letting sex blind him to all the differences between
them and shine some real life on the relationship. Let
him see for himself that there *was* no real relationship.
'I thought we'd go out for dinner.'

'Lovely.' Rather nervously, she looked at him. Apart
from that last night in France, it was the first time he'd
taken her out and she didn't want to let him down. 'Um,
is it somewhere very grand?'

'Actually, it's somewhere very un-grand,' he said
softly.

But surely his idea of 'un-grand' would still be fairly

posh? Zara's only job that day was a lunchtime business meeting in a vast loft in Soho—which gave her time to go shopping afterwards. She bought a silky green dress from one of the cut-price stores and a string of giant fake pearls and went back to Nikolai's house to get ready.

Going into the house was always a slightly daunting experience. She didn't have a key and she knew that his housekeeper disapproved of her—probably remembering her from the night she'd worked there, serving canapés. But she forced a bright smile as the older woman opened the door.

'Is Nikolai home yet?' asked Zara.

'Not yes, miss. Mr Komarov is expected shortly.'

Murmuring her thanks, Zara went upstairs, showered and made her face up and by the time Nikolai came home she was ready and dressed. He paused for a moment in the doorway of the bedroom, his eyes raking over her.

Green suited her, he thought—especially when it skimmed over her bottom like that and allowed him to see a great deal of her spectacular thighs.

'Why, you look magnificent, *angel moy*,' he said softly as he pulled off his tie.

'Do I?' She was about to tell him that it was only a cheap dress but then stopped herself. A woman should always keep *something* back—and mightn't he think that she was hinting he buy her something more expensive?

'Mmm. Completely delectable. In fact, I don't think I'd better risk kissing you in case I change my mind about going out—so give me ten minutes to get changed.'

His car took them to a restaurant in Shoreditch which overlooked the Regent's Park canal—but the air was sultry and heavy as they stepped onto the baking pavement and Zara wondered if they were due a storm. It was a very simple venue—a large room with scrubbed wooden floors and tables and bare walls—so that all the attention was focused on the green-grey water of the canal which slid past the giant windows. The menu was simple, too—much of the food grown on nearby allotments, according to the enthusiastic young waitress who served them. They ordered risotto cooked with courgette flowers and a big, herby green salad.

'This wasn't the kind of place I was expecting,' said Zara as she took a sip of red wine which tasted of raspberries.

'And what kind of place were you expecting?'

'Oh, I don't know.' She looked around at the blackboard and the wire basket of lemons on the bar. 'Somewhere more in the centre of town, I suppose—with crisp white tablecloths and candles and gleaming crystal.'

'Is that what you would have preferred?'

Something dark in his tone unsettled her and she put down her fork and stared at him, her heart beating very fast. 'We're not back onto the gold-digger theme, are we, Nikolai?

'Of course not. I was simply asking a question.'

Was he? She never really knew what he was thinking—just as she sometimes felt she didn't know him at all. All she ever saw of him were the bits he wanted her to see—the veneer he presented to the world. He was like one of those painting-by-numbers kits she used to have as a child, the picture all grey and indistinct—until portions of it gradually came to life with the addition of various bits of colour. But he gave her no colour to play with, she realised—and maybe she was going to have to dig deeper and find some for herself.

'No, I would not have preferred somewhere like

that—I work in places like that. I like it here. It's different—and I like the simplicity.' She ran her fingertip around the edge of her wine glass. 'Do you have restaurants like this in Russia?'

'Of course we do. There are restaurants like this all over the world. But only in affluent areas will you find peasant food which comes with a mighty price-tag,' he commented wryly. 'That's one of the many ironies of life, Zara. Those who have known hardship try to recreate it once they have escaped from its clutches.'

'I hadn't thought of it like that.' Her fingertip halted and she looked up into his eyes. 'Have you known hardship, then?' she questioned softly.

His eyes narrowed. 'What's this, the beginning of an interrogation?'

'Interrogation?' She put her glass down. 'That's a slightly heavy way to put it! I can't deny being interested in your life—why wouldn't I be when we've been spending so much time together—and, besides, you wanted to know about mine, didn't you?'

Idly, he swirled the red wine in his glass. Maybe her question was another subconscious warning that, essentially, women were all the same. That deep down they wanted to bleed you dry—and if it wasn't materially, then it was emotionally.

He took a sip of wine, aware that he hadn't yet changed the subject with the seamless skill for which he was known when anyone tried to stray too close. Was that because there was something about Zara which made him less inclined to be dismissive about his past? She was not the usual type of woman he had an affair with. She was poor, for a start, yet she was fiercely independent in spite of that. He suspected that she was honourable, too, and much too decent a person to use any private information against him when their affair eventually ended.

Besides, some of his background was already on the record—he supposed that he should be grateful she hadn't already hit the search engine of her computer to try to find out about him. But nobody had ever managed to put flesh on the bones of his past…and wasn't talking about a subject he kept so firmly off-limits more than a little tempting?

'Yes, I've known hardship,' he said slowly. 'I grew up in a time and a place where hunger and poverty were commonplace.'

A fragment of something he'd once said floated back to her. 'Did you lose your parents when you were very young…in some kind of accident?'

His eyes narrowed. 'Why do you ask that?'

'I just thought…' She remembered the sudden flash of understanding in his eyes when she'd told him about her parents being killed. Hadn't part of her thought that it might have been some sort a shared bond between them? Two people who'd been formed by tragedy. She shook her head. 'Nothing.'

Nikolai took a bigger mouthful of wine, wondering why he had ever agreed to go down this road. The wine was rich, and strong—it should have been relaxing were it not for the subject which now reared up from the past, like an ugly spectre. For wasn't there part of him which wished his parents *had* been killed in some tragic accident—which would have allowed him to remember them with fondness and love, instead of anger?

And shouldn't Zara hear that? Wouldn't it make her understand why he could never be the man he suspected she wanted him to be? A normal, rounded guy who was eager to create a family unit of his own. 'I never knew my father,' he said quietly. 'But being illegitimate certainly wasn't unusual in Moscow in those days. And neither was being hungry.'

He found himself recalling the lines of shabby washing flapping at the front of the high-rise flats. The kitchen and the bathroom shared with three other families. The food eaten at speed—as if fearful that it might be snatched from your plate. It had taken him a long time to learn how to eat slowly.

'And your mother?' questioned Zara tentatively.

'Ah. My mother.' His mouth hardened and he felt the painful lurch of his heart. 'My mother could never quite get used to hunger. When your stomach is empty it dominates your world—and she had envisaged a life where there were greater preoccupations than where the next meal was coming from. She was beautiful, you see. Extraordinarily beautiful. I don't think she could ever quite believe the cards that fate had dealt her. In another time and another place she probably would have risen effortlessly on looks alone. The trouble is that poverty and a fast-growing child do not tend to be great enhancers of beauty. And she was perceptive enough to see a window of opportunity she needed to take, before her looks faded.'

He shook his head as the waitress approached their table. 'So she travelled to England.'

'To *England*? You mean you were brought up in England?'

Nikolai realised that he had opened a door and invited Zara to look inside…what he hadn't realised was how much it could still hurt. If he could have taken his preceding words back, he would have done so in an instant—but he was in too far now to slam the door shut again. 'No. I was left behind in Moscow with my aunt and her boyfriend while my mother came here to earn what money she could to make our lives more bearable.'

There was a pause. A pause so full of raw emotion that Zara could barely breathe. She saw the pain in his eyes and flinched, but she knew that she couldn't shy away. Not now. 'What…what happened?'

There was another pause, but this time when he spoke his voice was flat, and Zara thought he didn't sound like a man at all—but one of those machines which spoke people's weight.

'Nothing happened. Oh, there used to be a card at Christmas and every year she remembered my birthday. But she never came back to Moscow and she never sent the money she promised, either. And I found that living with a drunken aunt and her wastrel of a partner was more than I could endure.' He gave a bitter laugh, pushed his plate away.

'I left Russia as soon as I could earn enough money for the fare—and I went to America, where I had been told that hard work would bring its own reward. For two years I worked in construction and salted away every cent I could. Eventually, I bought a property—a complete wreck of a place, but I could see its potential. Every hour I could spare, I worked on that house and I made a killing when I sold it—so I bought another. And then another. One day I discovered that I had a talent for speculation and so I began to play the markets—and when the money started to come in I diversified my portfolio into aluminium and telecommunications. It was the very best investment I could have made and I poured the profits into revitalising a big store which was on the decline. One store led to another and the rest, as they say, is history.'

Zara stared at him. His rise from rags to riches was impressive—but surely he had missed out the most important part of the story? 'And your mother? What happened to your mother?'

The temperature in the air seemed suddenly to plunge and there was a long moment before he chipped out the icy words. 'I never saw my mother again.'

For a moment Zara felt her heart lurch in shock as she stared at him in disbelief. 'What, *never*?'

A steely quality entered his voice but part of him could have shaken her for her damned persistence. 'Once I had the wherewithal, I tracked her down. I discovered that she'd found herself a wealthy lover—and that she'd been living with him on his estate in Oxfordshire all that time. It seemed that she'd put him first all along. That her son counted for nothing.' There was a pause. 'Soon after that, word reached me that she'd died.'

'Oh, Nikolai.' She tried to imagine the poor, lonely little boy he must have been—waiting for his mother to return. Waiting for money to arrive and lift him out of poverty, and the comfort of her arms around him. But he had been bitterly disappointed on both counts. How bewildered he must have been, she thought as she reached out and laid her hand over his on the table, but he did not return her tentative caress. 'That's terrible.'

'Maybe. But it is what it is. A therapist I once dated told me that my mother's behaviour was responsible for my "careless" attitude towards women. She said it explained why I was such a cold, heartless bastard.' He gave a short, humourless laugh. It hadn't stopped the woman from trying to get into his bed at every available opportunity, of course—or to persuade him that she wanted to have his baby. And it had taught him a very important lesson: *never date therapists*.

'Nikolai—'

But he shook his head. 'And do you know something? She was right. I *am* a cold-hearted bastard,' he said. 'I can go only so far, but no further. I don't *do* love. I don't want to marry—and I certainly don't want children of my own. And neither—' his ice-blue eyes now glittered out a distinct message '—do I want some woman on a mission—however sweet and sexy she might be—thinking that she's going to change my mind for me. Do you understand what I'm saying to you, Zara?'

She thought that you would have needed to be completely dense not to have understood the meaning which he had just hammered home so ruthlessly. And even though her heart clenched with a terrible feeling of disappointment she tried to tell herself that it was better to know the facts. He wasn't spinning her stories and making her build him up in her head and her heart. He was warning her. Showing her where the boundaries lay. Telling her not to fall for him because to do so would be pointless. *I don't do love*, he had said unequivocally—and nothing could be clearer than that.

Staring at the question in his ice-blue eyes, she nodded. 'Of course I do.'

'And that if we are to carry on seeing one another, you have to realise that I mean it. That there isn't going to be some miraculous conversion or change of heart.'

If we are to carry on seeing one another. If. Zara looked down at her hand, which still covered his. It was such a tiny word—but such a powerful one. He was laying down his terms, she realised. Just as he would do a business acquisition. 'Yes, I can see that you do mean it,' she said quietly.

'I can offer you a great deal, Zara—and if you want to continue with the arrangement we have, then nothing would please me more. You make a great—if somewhat unconventional—mistress. But I'll never marry you—and I'll never give you a baby. I'm sorry.' His gaze was very cool and very steady. 'I can't offer you long-term security, and if you want any of those things, then you'd better walk away right now and find it with someone else.'

Zara bit her lip. His words were harsh and brutal, but clearly that was his intention—just to be sure that there was no misunderstanding. She could be his mistress, yes—with all the pleasure that offered—but only if she was prepared to make the biggest sacrifice any woman could be asked to make. To kiss goodbye to the chance of having children as long as she stayed with him.

'You're very quiet,' he said softly.

'That was a bit of a bombshell. Actually, quite a big bombshell.'

There was a pause as his eyes seared into her. 'And?'

For a moment, she didn't answer. Nobody could say he hadn't been honest with her—but was honesty enough? Would she be settling for a situation which would ultimately break her heart—and wouldn't a sensible person end it now, before she got in any deeper?

But as her eyes drank in the angles and shadows of his sculpted features, Zara knew that she had neither the strength nor the inclination to end it. What had started out as fierce physical attraction between them had grown into something she'd neither wanted nor expected. And tonight he had peeled away some of the layers which made him such an indomitable force. She had seen through to the core of the man who lay beneath. A man with his own vulnerabilities and heartache.

And somewhere along the way, she realised, she'd fallen in love with that man.

She realised something else, too. That deep down she wanted to be cherished—just as she one day wanted to be a mother. She just hadn't known until that precise moment how much she wanted it. And Nikolai had just told her that he could never give it to her.

So what was it that made her pin a bright smile to her lips and to utter words which were fundamentally flawed? Was her love for him stronger than her desire for security, and a family? It seemed that maybe it was.

'I don't care about marriage or children, Nikolai,' she said. 'I'm happy just being with you.'

CHAPTER ELEVEN

'You haven't forgotten that we're going out to dinner tonight, *milaya moya*?'

Zara zipped up her black uniform skirt and turned round to look at Nikolai, aware that he'd been watching her get dressed, which seemed to be one of his favourite occupations. A striptease in reverse, he called it—and said it turned him on almost as much as the traditional variety. But then, pretty much everything turned Nikolai on...

'No, I haven't forgotten,' she said as she slipped a foot into the rubber-soled black soles which all Gourmet International staff had to wear. 'It's someone you know from when you lived in America, right?'

'That's right. We worked in construction together.' He gave a ghost of a smile. 'He's a senator now.' He frowned as she fiddled with the waistband of her skirt. 'I wish you weren't going to work today. I don't have meetings until later this morning, and...'

'And?' she questioned as his words tailed off and his eyes sent out a speculative message.

'We could have spent the morning in bed.'

'We can spend the morning in bed tomorrow— it's Saturday and I've got the whole weekend off, re- member?'

'That wasn't what I meant and you know it,' he growled. 'I meant that I don't like you going out to work.'

'I have to.'

He felt a flicker of irritation. 'Not really, Zara. I can easily support you.'

Zara smiled. Of course he could. He could probably support the entire staff of Gourmet International on a fraction of his income if he wanted to, but that wasn't the point. He'd *told* her that there was no permanence in this arrangement of theirs and Zara knew that she had to keep something of her independence. Because if she allowed Nikolai to take over her life completely, then what on earth would happen when the relationship finally fizzled out?

True, she would always be able to find a waitressing job—because waitressing jobs were fairly easy to come by—but lately she had begun to realise that maybe she wanted something more than just serving other people. And hadn't the impermanence of her relationship with Nikolai made her look at the bigger picture of her life and start wondering about her future? Perhaps she should look into the possibility of going back to agricultural college—or at least go and talk to somebody about it.

'We've had that discussion lots of times,' she said smoothly. 'And I've given you my views on it. I need to work—not just for the money, but for me. For my self-respect.'

'How stubborn you can be,' he mocked.

Zara smiled. 'You just don't like it because you're used to getting your own way!'

'Perhaps.' He let his gaze flicker over her feet. Funny how she could even look sexy in those horrible shoes she wore for work. 'But the dinner tonight *will* be grand,' he said carefully.

The unmistakable inference didn't escape her. 'Meaning that there's nothing in my wardrobe which is really suitable?'

'I'd hate you to feel awkward. Especially when it's so easy to fix.' There was a pause and he glittered her a look. 'So are you going to let me buy you something pretty to wear?'

He would have tempted a saint, but Zara shook her head. She'd never thought she'd end up being the mistress of a wealthy man and she was determined to escape the stereotype. That scarlet bikini he'd bought her in France had been the only thing he *had* bought her. She'd sketched out certain boundaries for herself, and she didn't want to feel like a kept woman. *And wasn't she aware that part of him would despise her if she just soaked up his generosity with little thought to the consequences?* He was bitter enough about his own mother falling prey to the lure of wealth, and she suspected that he longed to tar all women by the same brush. 'No, thanks. I'll ask Emma if I can wear one of her creations.'

'Ah, yes—your friend, the designer. Has she been in touch with my New York store yet?'

'She has. I told you the other evening but I didn't think you were listening.'

'That's because you always distract me, *angel moy.*'

'Well, she says to thank you and that they've asked to see some more of her designs.' She smiled. 'So I take it you won't mind if I model one of them tonight?'

For a moment he didn't answer as he pulled a silk tie from the drawer. Actually, yes, he *did* mind—and it had nothing to do with her modelling her friend's clothes. It was Zara's general resistance to letting him pay which was irritating the hell out of him. Yes, he admired her independence, but hadn't she made her point by now?

He'd got the message that she wasn't with him for his money—but she was taking pride onto a whole new level. Why, even on her birthday last week, when he'd twisted her arm and taken her to a fancy jeweller's, she had shunned the gleaming pearl necklace he'd offered to buy her, and opted for a new watch instead. Even that had been less than satisfactory. He'd never known a woman refuse an exquisite diamond-studded gold watch strap and opt for a plain leather band on the grounds that it was more practical. But Zara had.

'I don't see why you insist on being so stubborn.'

'Don't you? Think about it, darling—you're an intelligent man!' She gave him a soft smile. 'Don't you think we should try and keep the balance of power between us as equal as possible? It isn't always easy, but I'm doing my best.'

He felt wrong-footed—infuriatingly so—even though he understood her reasoning perfectly. But Nikolai was hard-wired to control and to dominate—and Zara's refusal to let him call all the shots was robbing him of that dominance. Did she imagine that stubborn pride would win his heart? he wondered grimly. Surely she could not be *that* naïve?

'As you wish,' he said coolly, bending to give her only the briefest of kisses. 'I'll see you later.'

But his cool reaction left Zara with a slightly unsettled feeling—even when she made it to Emma's studio and discovered that her friend was delighted to lend her a scarlet silk dress which would be perfect for the event.

'How's life with lover-boy?' Emma questioned curiously. 'Mum says you always dash off as soon as your shift's over and never stay behind for a drink. Can't wait to get back to him, I suppose? Not that I blame you, of course. If I had a man like Nikolai waiting at home, I don't think I'd ever set foot outside the house.'

Zara frowned as she considered her friend's words. Had she been neglecting her work friends because of her obsession with her Russian lover? Maybe she *should* join them all for a drink next week. 'It's...it's wonderful.'

'Is it really?' asked Emma sagely. 'Is that why you're starting to get frown lines on your brow or why I'm having to take in this dress at the waist?'

Zara stared into the unforgiving mirror, taken aback by faint shadows beneath her cheekbones and the loose fabric which was bunched in Emma's hand. *Had* she lost weight? Probably. But didn't all women lose weight when they began a love affair?

Her friend's words still mocked her as she took the dress and shoes back to Nikolai's Kensington mansion and began to get ready for dinner. But her heart was heavy as she pulled on silk stockings after her shower— as if she had suddenly become aware of the things missing from her life. Maybe it was time she confronted the truth instead of dodging it. Started seeing things as they really were and not how she wanted them to be. And this...*relationship* between them seemed to be going nowhere, did it?

Because despite his warnings that he didn't want marriage or babies or that he didn't 'do' love, that hadn't stopped Zara hoping that he might change his mind, had it? Hoping that Nikolai might start to feel something deeper for her, too. Because that was what women did. They hoped and they dreamed, no matter how much the odds were stacked against them.

She pushed her troubled thoughts aside as the car took them to the dinner. The red silk dress fitted like a dream and Zara was grateful she'd worn it because Nikolai had been right: it was certainly a very grand occasion. She was seated on the opposite side of the table, several feet away from her lover, and she found herself watching him almost objectively as he made the senator's wife roar with laughter. She realised that he had an abundance of charm he could use when it suited him—and it suited him to do so tonight.

She saw the way that people hung onto his every word—men *and* women, but especially women. She heard the rather sycophantic way they laughed at his jokes, while her own conversation to her neighbours was greeted with polite indifference. Didn't matter how engaging or witty she was, nobody was interested in her. She was just Nikolai's accessory—his current bed partner with no status and only a limited shelf-life.

And suddenly the reality of her watered-down existence hit home as she tried to imagine what was going to happen to them, as a couple. Only this time her vision wasn't clouded by wishful thinking as she recognised that it would just be more of the same—the intensity of their relationship gradually diminishing as initial passion burnt itself out.

She remembered when he'd made love to her in the south of France—how she'd felt like one of his puppets—well, what had changed? Absolutely nothing. This wasn't really living, she realised—it was pretending. It was closing her eyes to what lay ahead of her.

She had carried on waitressing because the undemanding work suited her current lifestyle—conveniently ignoring the fact that before she'd met him she had been thinking of doing something else with her life. He had laid down his rules and she had eagerly agreed to abide by them because she was in love with him. Had she perhaps thought that her love plus a little independence might be enough to make him soften his stance a little? Even though he'd explicitly warned her not to, hadn't she hoped that he might change his mind about marriage, and children? Well, she had been wrong—and unless she had the courage to try to change things, then her frustration would grow and grow.

Questions she'd never dared ask him began to bubble up inside her as they made their way home but she waited until they were in his vast bedroom. Waited until he had made love to her and they lay, sleepy and sated against the rumpled bedding, with the glowing lamps throwing pools of pale amber light onto the polished floor.

She turned onto her stomach and lay her head on his chest.

'Nikolai?'

'Mmm?' He picked up a strand of her silky hair and wound it around his finger.

'Can I ask you something?'

He turned his head to look at her, his eyes narrowing. 'Now why does that kind of question always make my heart sink?'

She heard the unmistakable warning contained in his careless response but Zara had spent hours plucking up the courage to do this. She *needed* to do this. Gently, she stroked the side of his face. 'Did you ever find out what your mother's life had been like in England? Did you…did you ever go to Oxfordshire to try to discover more about what had happened to her?'

Nikolai stiffened, aware of the sudden race of his heart. 'What's brought this up all of a sudden?'

'Does it matter?'

'Actually, it does. It matters that you've seen fit to spoil a perfectly good evening by dragging up something which is none of your business.'

Zara bit her lip as she heard the abrasiveness in his voice. 'Can't I ask a question without you flying off the handle?'

'But your very question implies that I've been neglectful in some way!' he declared. 'What do you think I should have done? Turned up on her doorstep and said, "Look, I know you left years ago and broke all your promises to me—but I'm longing to meet the man who made you turn your back on your only child."' His mouth curved with contempt. 'Is that what you think, Zara?'

Much of it was hidden behind a blaze of anger, but the pain in his eyes was very real and Zara knew that she couldn't let up—not now. 'Nothing's ever as black and white as it sometimes seems,' she whispered. 'You don't know what your mother had to face when she came over here.'

'What's this, a spirited defence of women in general, or her in particular—a woman you never even met but now see fit to judge?'

'It's neither!' she said, recoiling from the icy fury in his eyes and feeling tentative hope wither inside her. 'It's the realisation that I've suddenly come to my senses—and I can't be involved with someone who doesn't allow himself to feel *anything*! Who pushes uncomfortable topics away rather than confront them.'

'But I told you what I was like at the beginning, Zara.'

'I know you did. I know.' She gave a heavy sigh. 'And I thought that I could accept it. But I was wrong, Nikolai. I can't.'

His eyes narrowed. 'So is this leading to some kind of ultimatum you've been cooking up? You threaten to leave me and hope that the diamond ring and promise of commitment comes swinging your way? As a strategy, I have to tell you that it's been used before—but it never works.'

There was a moment of stunned silence while she stared at him, realising that her fierce determination to remain as independent as possible had gone unnoticed. Nikolai had never really revised his opinion of her, had he? To him, all women were deceitful gold-diggers and nothing was ever going to rid him of that notion.

'My God,' she breathed. 'You're even more cold-hearted than I thought. You think that I'd actively choose to share my life with a man who is so sparing with his affection? Are you labouring under the illusion that your wealth somehow makes up for your emotional deficiencies? Well, in that case—you don't have a clue! And maybe I'd better leave you to your suspicious little world, Nikolai—because I'm finding the atmosphere in it too *stifling* to stay!'

Her heart hammering, she leapt from the bed and began scrabbling around to find some clothes, pulling on a pair of jeans and a sweater which she kept in a couple of the drawers she'd been allocated.

Nikolai didn't move, just lay in bed—watching her—like some brooding golden statue.

'Where do you think you're going?'

She pulled out her small bag from the bottom of the wardrobe and hurled a handful of knickers inside it. 'Home!'

'Not in the middle of the night, you're not.'

'This is London. It's a twenty-four-hour *city*! And we do have cabs!'

'I think you're completely overreacting but if you're hell bent on this ridiculous display of hysteria, then you will take my car,' he bit out furiously.

'I will not!' she flared back, bitterly aware that he

wasn't doing anything to stop her. 'And I am not over-reacting! Can you please have the rest of my things sent round in the morning?'

'With pleasure!' he grated, his eyes blazing at hers in icy challenge—as if *daring her* to go through with it. And to his astonishment and fury, he saw her pick up her bag and turn her back on him!

Zara ran from the room and down the sweeping stair-case—but it took her so long to undo the triple-locked front door that by the time she'd opened it, Nikolai's driver was standing outside waiting for her. She thought for a moment about brushing past him and telling him that she could make her own way home, thank you very much. But the realisation that it was late made common sense override her pride as she climbed into the back of the luxurious car. She glanced up at the house to see Nikolai's bedroom light snapping off, so that the house lay in darkness—and she felt a great tide of rage swelling up inside her. He had actually *gone back to sleep*! Cold-hearted, unfeeling *robot* of a man!

But once her anger had died down, regret began to rush in to replace it. Wasn't it strange that, having made her escape, she now began to wonder if she'd been too hasty? Why, if she'd kept her stupid mouth shut, she could have been tucked up beside him in bed and by the morning the whole thing would have been forgotten.

Except that it wouldn't be, would it? Not really. All she would have done would have been to bury the prob-lem a little deeper—but it wasn't going to go away unless one of them addressed it. And it certainly wasn't going to be him—because Nikolai didn't see it as a problem. He had no desire to seek out the answer to questions from his past and couldn't see how much that was impacting on the present.

The driver dropped her off at her little house and after she'd made herself some herb tea, Zara went upstairs to bed. But she was much too restless to sleep—even if the sound of traffic and drinkers heading home from the pub hadn't made such a racket. It seemed ages since she'd stayed in this tiny bedroom of hers and she thought how quickly she had adapted to her wealthy lover's quiet and privileged lifestyle.

Well, it was better to be free of it now. Yes, it would hurt—but not nearly so much as if she kept postponing it. What if she'd spent months as his mistress? Years, even? And then one day he'd turned round to her and told her that he'd found a replacement? Because that was what rich men did, wasn't it? She remembered Sergei with his laughably young partner and, restlessly, she turned her pillow over to lay her heated cheek against it.

Next morning she went out into the garden and could have wept at the sad neglect of her godmother's little vegetable patch. Tomato plants had toppled from their canes and broad beans were covered thickly in black-fly. All that time and work and care which had been poured into cultivating the small London garden now lay wasted and Zara felt ashamed. Why, she hadn't so much as picked up a fork or a spade for weeks. It was if she hadn't been able to wait to shrug off her old life and embrace the new one.

Coming from inside the kitchen, she heard the sound of her cell-phone ringing and when she went to answer it she saw the name *Nikolai* flashing on the screen. And even though an inner voice urged her to ignore it—wasn't it telling that she paid it no attention? Because wasn't she longing to speak to him—secretly praying that the stupid row could be resolved?

'Hello, Nikolai.'

'So have you calmed down this morning?'

Zara swallowed. 'If that remark was designed to placate me then I have to tell you that it has failed dismally.'

'I am not trying to *placate* you!' he bit out. 'Just to ask whether you are intending to be sensible and to come back?'

Sensible? Now he was making her sound like some overexcited schoolgirl who had thrown an unreasonable hissy-fit! 'And then what?'

Nikolai gave a long sigh. *Don't make this any more difficult than it already is,* he urged her silently. Didn't she realise that even asking her to come back had been hard enough and that part of him still couldn't believe he was doing it? 'Then we carry on as we are, Zara—just as we've been doing. We have a good time together. We're good for each other.' His voice dipped. 'You know we are.'

'But that's where you're wrong,' she whispered, steeling herself against the sultry caress in his voice. 'We're good at all the externals and we're good in bed—but it's not enough. Relationships are supposed to grow, Nikolai—not stay packed in ice.'

His voice was silky-soft. 'I thought I told you that I would not tolerate any kind of ultimatum.'

'And I'm not making one! I'm just telling you that I don't want to live your life any more.'

'Really? And just what kind of life is that?' he demanded dangerously.

'One which is superficial. One where things get replaced when the novelty and the gloss has worn off them.'

'Perhaps you'd care to elaborate since I'm not entirely sure what it is you're accusing me of?' he demanded even as the knuckles of his clenched fist whitened with anger.

'What about your friend Sergei with his decades-younger girlfriend?' she questioned shakily. 'Is that how you see yourself in the future? Thinking that once my appeal has faded you'll replace me with a newer, shinier version and then eventually you'll replace my replace-ment. Until one day you wake up as a fifty-something man in bed with a woman who's young enough to be his daughter?'

'How *dare* you speak to me this way?'

'The fact that you feel you have the right to ask that question is answer enough! I dare because I've realised that I *am* your equal, Nikolai! Oh, not in money or in material things or anything like that, but under the skin we're exactly the same—two human beings with the right to an honest, decent life. You've decided that you don't want to find out more about your mother—well, that's your choice. But that decision has impacted on everything else in your life. You're never going to be able to trust a woman and I'm not going to pussyfoot around your feelings any more—simply because you got lucky and made yourself a fortune!'

'Got *lucky*?' he stormed. '*Got lucky!* I worked damned hard to get to where I am today!'

'Lots of us work hard, darling—but we don't all end up as billionaires!'

He said something furious in Russian and cut the connection, hurling the phone down so that it skidded like a novice ice-skater across the desk, before pacing over to the window of his vast office. Who the *hell* did she think she was, talking to him like that? Some little nobody of a waitress whom he'd picked out and offered the opportunity of a lifetime. Yet what had she done to thank him? Nothing! Only thrown everything back in his face and added a few choice insults into the bargain. He glowered out at the London skyline, telling himself he was well rid of her.

That evening he attended a party he'd been intending to miss—after deciding it might be good for him. It was held in a lavish six-storey town house in Notting Hill and was attended by politicians and media people, with a large smattering of stars from the world of showbiz and the accompanying bank of paparazzi waiting outside.

The music was achingly trendy, the wine superb and the air buzzed with the indefinable sound of success. A beautiful French actress made a beeline for him and he found himself assessing her dispassionately as she smiled up at him. He admired her petite figure in the sleek Chanel dress and the towering black patent shoes which complemented it. He thought she was rather beautiful— with her glossy twist of raven hair and full lips and that way which actresses had of making you feel as if you were the only man in their universe when they fixed you in the spotlight of their gaze.

But he drank barely a single glass of champagne as he listened to her. When he turned to leave, she asked whether he might drop her home and it seemed churlish to refuse—even though they had to dodge the battery of photographers on the way to the car. But he turned down her invitation to join her for a nightcap—despite her promises of a wonderful night-time view from her balcony. He bit back a wry smile. He'd been offered views like that in the past—and rarely did they involve any kind of sky-watching. Instead, he said goodnight and leaned back in his seat, his eyes closed as his car took him home to Kensington.

At least work had always been his saviour and he

began to devote more time to projects already in the pipeline. He tackled new mergers with alacrity and injected more funds into his long-running research to find greener energy supplies. A plot of land he'd acquired in Moscow was being developed as a day-centre and crèche for single mothers and he promised them he would pay it another visit soon.

But through it all he felt a strange kind of *emptiness*—as if someone had punched a big gaping hole inside him—and he didn't like it. He didn't like it one bit. Angrily, he told himself that he wasn't going to let any woman get underneath his skin, particularly the kind of woman who hadn't learnt when to keep silent and be grateful for what she'd got. Was that what significant women always did? he wondered bitterly. Made themselves important in your life so that it hurt like hell when they left you?

He spent two weeks with his head pounding with questions he had no desire to answer and he pushed them away with a ruthless certainty which made him furious when they kept coming back. Every morning he awoke with an aching body and cursed the day he had ever set eyes on Zara Evans with her come-to-bed eyes and a distinctive brand of honesty which should have sent him running in the opposite direction. Damn her sweet seductive body, he thought—and the way that a man could lose himself inside all its slick, secret places.

Until one day he realised that he simply couldn't go on like this any more.

And that was the day he picked up the telephone.

CHAPTER TWELVE

SUNLIGHT caught the sparkling stream of water which Zara directed onto the parched earth from the metal watering can. There had been no rain for days now, and the neglected vegetables had taken much more effort than she'd anticipated. Morning and evening she'd been outside whenever work had allowed—trimming and snipping, and pinching side shoots from the tomato plants so that the fruits could grow bigger. The tangled jungle had retreated and daily routine had restored some sort of order to the little plot. Now it looked more like the place she used to come home to—where she and her godmother would sit outside in deckchairs on warm summer evenings and eat newly picked strawberries and raspberries still warm from the cane. What a long time ago those distant days of childhood seemed.

But she was grateful for the garden. Warm earth and encroaching weeds were a great distraction from thinking about Nikolai. Sometimes she even managed to go for a whole half-hour without him being on her mind. And it was at times like this that she wished she had a more demanding job—something that would require all her attention instead of only part of it—because it was all too easy to daydream when you were standing around, waiting for people to finish their pudding.

It was going to bed she dreaded most of all—because it was there that she remembered the way he'd held her and stroked her hair. In the silent, empty hours of the night it was bittersweet to recall his slow kisses and the powerful physical intimacy which had existed between them.

Sometimes she wondered if she had been too hasty in walking away from him—but the pain of missing him was quickly replaced with the realisation that the price of being with Nikolai was too high. For a man to warn a woman that she could never carry his child nor wear his ring. To tell her that his heart would always be empty and cold—how could any woman bear that?

The sound of the doorbell interrupted her painful thoughts and she put down the watering can, wiping her hands on the front of her jeans as she went to answer it. Maybe it was one of the neighbours—or Emma paying another 'surprise' visit, which was nothing but a thinly disguised attempt to get Zara to eat more.

But it wasn't Emma who stood there—nor one of the neighbours. Instead, Zara's heart missed a beat as she saw Nikolai Komarov filling most of the tiny doorframe.

Little spots danced in front of her eyes as the ice-blue eyes and angled features blazed into her line of vision. He was dressed very casually, in jeans and a T-shirt. She had done precious little else other than think of him in the days since they'd been apart, but the reality of seeing him again took her breath away and her heart was hammering so hard that she felt quite dizzy.

'Hello, Zara,' he said.

'Nikolai.' The word seemed to stick in her throat, like a fishbone—but she swallowed down her nerves. 'This is a surprise.'

'Is it?' His eyes glittered her a question. 'Didn't you think you'd see me again?'

'I'm not sure what I thought.'

'Can I come in?'

'Of…of course.'

He stepped over the threshold and followed her into the sitting room. He hadn't been here since that night when he'd stormed in to find out why she'd ripped his cheque into a thousand tiny pieces. Actually, that wasn't quite true. He had come here that night, blazing with sexual desire and a determination to carry her off to make wild and passionate love to her. And she had resisted, he recalled wryly as he remembered her refusal to go home with him. It seemed that one way or another she had always been resisting him all along. And hadn't that refusal to bend to his will been one of the things which had made her so irresistible to him, even though it had infuriated the hell out of him?

'Would you…?' Zara was feeling nervous and aching with longing, which she hid behind a careful smile. *Be polite*, she told herself. *Even if you're destined to be nothing but ex-lovers, at least you can be civilised about it.* 'Like a drink?'

He raised his eyebrows. 'Not the orange liqueur?'

'Actually, there's white wine in the fridge. Or I've got some home-made lemonade, if you'd prefer. We could drink it in the garden.'

He shrugged. 'Why not?'

Stepping outside into the little yard, he took in the scene before him. He had judged her humble house by the quality of the nearby dwellings but out here he found an unexpected oasis of green. Vegetables and soft fruits sprouted prolifically and the scarlet gleam of tomatoes hung heavy on the thick-stemmed plants. In a way it reminded him of Russia, where people used to cultivate every spare centimetre of land in order to grow food. In the midst of all this tangled green was a small wrought-iron table and a couple of chairs and he sat down on one.

The tinkling of ice announced her appearance and Nikolai watched as she carried the tray into the garden, creating a bizarre, snapshot image of rural life in the heart of the city. For the first time he could imagine her as the agricultural student she'd once been—with her long legs encased in mud-dusted denim and her thick hair piled up on top of her head. Tendrils of it fell down untidily about her flushed cheeks and he realised she wasn't wearing a scrap of make-up. For the first time, it occurred to him that maybe the reason Zara hadn't leapt on the chance to wear the silk and jewels he'd offered her was because that image wasn't really *her*. That it was more than a stubborn refusal to be bought or controlled by a man—but a sense of not wanting to submerge her own identity in his.

She leaned over to pour him some lemonade and he could see a trickle of sweat meandering down her neck, towards her breasts. He wanted to lick it off and he wanted to tell her that he'd never drunk home-made lemonade before. He shook his head very slightly as he accepted a glass from her. Was he losing his mind—or simply light-headed from the beat of the sun and the hard ache in his groin?

'So.' Zara pulled out the other chair and sat facing him. This was weird. More than weird. She'd always comforted herself with the thought that Nikolai would never have been comfortable if their lives had ever over-lapped, but the irony was that at that moment he looked as if he had been born to sit in her tiny garden. His long legs were stretched out in front of him, his dark gold hair was all ruffled and there was a terrible tearing pain in her heart as she realised how much she wanted to go up and sit on his lap and kiss him. But he didn't look remotely in the mood for kissing and his guarded expression made a thousand questions crowd into her mind. 'Why are you here?'

'Because I took your advice.'

'You took my advice?' she repeated slowly.

He acknowledged her surprise. If it came as a shock to her, it had come as an even greater one to him. If anyone had told him that he would have given her words careful consideration—even while part of him had kicked against it—he'd never have believed them. But he had. 'I thought about what you said about laying ghosts to rest.' There was a pause. 'And realised that I needed to find out what happened to my mother.'

Zara stared at him—but could read no hint of what he had found in the enigmatic gleam of his eyes. 'And did you?'

'I did.' In the distance, he heard a woman shout to someone that dinner was ready and he thought about all the different ways that people lived their lives. He thought about his mother and about what he had discovered.

'She started out working in a salad-packing factory when she first came to England,' he said slowly. 'Which was the only job she could get. It was soulless work— long hours on a low wage—but it was still more than she could ever have earned in Moscow. Like her, the other women working there were all immigrants and they lived in cramped caravans on site. Sometimes they would travel to the nearby town on a Saturday for a night out—and it was there that she met a man.' There was a pause before he spoke again. 'He was older than her and enormously rich—and completely captivated by her beauty. She told him her story and he was touched that she was trying to make a better life for her little boy who was so far away. So he gave her extra money to send to me in Moscow.'

He met Zara's eyes and shrugged in answer to her unspoken question. 'By this time she was sleeping with him, yes—though from what I understand, it was a genuine love-match between the two of them. But it wasn't until he saw the size of her miserable bed in the damp caravan that he announced that he was buying them a house and taking her away from her life there.'

'You mean, she married him?'

There was another pause and this time she saw his mouth twist.

'That was never an option since her lover was already married,' he said heavily. 'And he told her from the outset that he had no intention of leaving his wife and children. In fact, the family home was in the very next town and he rarely spent a night with my mother.'

Now Zara was confused. 'So why did she stay? And why didn't she send the money to you?'

'She stayed because she was torn. She loved him, and the money was too good to turn her back on. She thought it would provide my life with a kick-start. And she *did* send me money—a great deal of it, in fact. The problem was that it never actually reached *me*.' His fists clenched; unclenched—the knuckles making a cracking sound as they whitened against his knees. 'My aunt and her partner siphoned off every ruble which came to the apartment and then drank most of it away. Worse than that, they destroyed most of her letters to me.'

'Oh, Nikolai.' Zara's hand flew to her mouth. 'That's absolutely terrible. What…what happened?'

He had known that her face would soften with sweet sympathy and hadn't a part of him longed for that—just as the other conflicting side of his nature had made him want to reject it? To tell her that he didn't need her sympathy. That he didn't need a damned thing from her.

'She died—quite suddenly—and when they went through her belongings, they found out that she'd spent years trying to get the authorities to allow me to join her.'

'But how….how did you discover all this?' she whispered.

'I tracked down her lover's son. He was surprisingly helpful—in fact, he was exceedingly generous, given the circumstances. He said his father had really loved my mother but that he'd owed the greater loyalty to his family. He took me to her grave. I,,,'

The faltering thickness of his voice was like a spear to her heart and Zara stood up and went to him, not caring about the state of their relationship or whether or not it was over. Not caring about anything other than a fierce need to reach out and comfort him. She put her arms around him, hugged him very tightly. 'I'm so sorry.'

For a moment he resisted and then he put his arms around her waist and rested his face on her breasts. 'How I have misjudged her,' he said bitterly.

'What else could you have done? You had no evidence of this—only the reality of your life. You were just a child—caught in a mixed-up world of adults with all their conflicting needs. How could you have known that you were a victim of your aunt's greed?' She sucked in a faltering breath before expelling it in a rush. 'But you've made your peace with her now, Nikolai.'

'How?' he demanded. 'How have I done that?'

'Because you've discovered the truth—that she was doing the best she could. And you've forgiven her. You have, haven't you? And now you will just have to learn to forgive yourself. That's what she would want. You must, Nikolai—or else all her efforts will have been in vain.' She lifted his face and bent to kiss it—staying very close when finally she drew her lips away. 'Mustn't you?' she questioned softly.

He knew she was right. Just as he knew he wouldn't have gone seeking the truth if it hadn't been for her. He would have just buried all the unanswered questions and let them eat away at him. He nodded. 'I owe you,' he said quietly.

'You don't owe me anything.'

'Yes, I do.' He just hadn't worked out how to pay off the debt. Wouldn't the best thing he could do for Zara Evans be to walk away from her and let this whole affair fade into a distant memory? Tightening his hands around her waist, he inhaled deeply and could smell the pungent scent of the tomato leaves on her skin as desire drove every good intention from him, bar the urgent need to possess her again. How could he bear to let her go when she could still make him feel like this? 'And I've missed you,' he said huskily.

'Well, that I *can* agree with. I've missed you, too.'

Roughly, he pulled her properly onto his lap, splayed his hand very deliberately over her breast. 'How much?'

'It's…' she felt her eyes close '…difficult to quantify.'

'We could try.'

'Yes, we could.'

He looked at her. 'Do you think we should resume where we left off?'

Every instinct in her body screamed at her to be careful. To protect herself against potential heartache. Because he wasn't offering her anything different, was he? Just more of the same. 'I don't know, Nikolai,' she whispered. 'I just don't know.'

'Don't you? I think you do.' He began to kiss her, lips brushing provocatively against hers until eventually they stayed there as the kiss lengthened, hardened. He slipped his hand underneath her T-shirt and a rush of heat swept through her as he began to caress her breast. A little cry escaped her as her hungry body flared into life beneath his touch. She was greedy for him. Impatient for him. Boldly, she let her fingers brush over the hardened ridge in his jeans until he sucked in an unsteady breath.

'If we don't move from here in a minute,' he ground out, 'then I think we're in danger of having an indecency order slapped on us.'

'You…' Her tongue edged out to moisten lips which suddenly seemed to have swollen to twice their normal size. 'You once boasted to me how discreet you could be.'

Had he? Yes, he had. In a car on a mountainside in France when his desire to possess her had been urgent. It was still urgent, but he no longer wanted to demonstrate his sleight of hand, nor to feel a heady sense of power at how easily he could pleasure a woman. He wanted her in the most fundamental way of all—to be deep inside her body—and here was not the place. 'No boasting now, *angel moy*. I am a reformed and humble man.'

Sure he was. With a wistful smile, Zara traced the outline of his lips with her finger. 'You w-want to go home?'

'Actually…' his voice was uneven '…I thought that I

might have a look at your bedroom now that I'm here. Do you want to show me where it is?'

'Oh, yes,' she whispered as the unbearable possibility of having to wait a moment longer began to recede.

It seemed somehow daring to lead him up the narrow staircase to the little room she'd had since childhood. She had modified it since then, of course—her jigsaw puzzles and toy farm had long been replaced by books and on the walls were blown-up photos she'd taken at college of misty, early-morning harvests and a much-prized moonlit shot of a deserted beach. But nobody had ever lain on this bed except for her and somehow the fact that it should be Nikolai felt terribly significant. Or was she reading too much into it—because she loved him—loved him in a way he had not asked to be loved?

Don't frighten him away, she told herself as she bit back the overwhelming desire to blurt the words out. Yet no matter how hard she tried to temper her feelings, Zara found herself overcome with emotion as he pulled the clips from her hair. In fact, she was so overcome that she just stood there, helpless and unmoving as he peeled off her T-shirt and her bra and pushed the jeans down her trembling legs so that she was left wearing nothing.

He tugged at his belt and impatiently shrugged off his own clothes and she was still trembling when he drew her down onto the bed and covered her with his mouth and his body.

'Zara,' he whispered.

His kisses were heated and his fingers roved hungrily over her breasts until he found even more intimate quarry and he gave a little moan as he encountered her slick heat and began to move rhythmically against it.

'I don't want to wait,' he declared.

'Then *don't*,' she urged him just as fiercely as she took the condom from him and began to slide it on. Her fingers were shaky and her movements imprecise and she heard him mutter something harsh and fervent in his native tongue.

'For God's sake,' he ground out. 'You're driving me crazy.'

'Do it to me, Nikolai,' she whispered. 'Do it to me *now*.'

The rising notes of her erotic plea splintered his composure as he thrust into her and she gasped as he entered her, just as deep as he could go. It felt so good, he realised distractedly as he filled her hot, tight heat. Better every time. He could feel his control slipping and concentrated instead on her little cries of pleasure which were accompanying every sweet thrust. These walls must be thin, he thought suddenly as he lowered his mouth to hers in a hard kiss which muffled the sound.

He moved on her. In her. Again and again he brought her to the brink until she was mindless with pleasure as she writhed beneath him. Her silken skin felt so cool and welcoming and he could taste the bittersweet taste of lemonade on her mouth. Taut nipples contrasted with the soft weight of her breasts as they pushed against him. And then, just when he thought he could not bear it for one second longer, her supple body began to arch beneath his. Like a marksman's bow, was his last conscious thought as his orgasm arrowed through him and he lifted his head and cried out.

Afterwards, they lay there, damp limbs tangled due to lack of space as Nikolai traced a little circle around the dip of her navel. Time seemed suspended and all

Zara could hear was the sound of his breathing and the muffled slowing of her own heartbeat.

'I think there had better be some changes in the future,' he said eventually.

She turned onto her side. 'Oh?'

'I'm giving you a key.'

'A key?' she echoed blankly.

'To my house. It's impractical for you to have to rely on the housekeeper every time you want to get in.' Didn't she realise the significance—he who had never given a woman a key before? And yet something made him wary of telling her—because it might be only a temporary measure. Probably *was* only a temporary measure. He'd be bored with her by the time the year was out—and she would probably be bored with him, too. 'And I want you in my house as much as possible, Zara.'

She stared at him. Surely giving her a key to his house was a small step forward—perhaps the first of many? Was Nikolai beginning to acknowledge that she *did* mean something to him? She kept her voice studiedly neutral. 'Do you?'

'Mmm. Preferably in my bed,' he murmured as he drifted his lips over her throat. 'You were born to grace my bed.'

Zara's smile didn't slip. What had she thought? That because she'd encouraged him to confront the truth of his past he would somehow come out with a great out-pouring of love and emotion? That just because he had been tender and sweet with her in the garden, it actually *meant* something? Tender and sweet was what men did when they wanted sex with a woman. And biting back feelings of insecurity was what women did when they loved a man… 'I guess I should say thank you.'

'Oh, I think you can show your thanks in other ways,

milaya moya.' He pushed a wayward strand of hair away from the tempting curve of her lips and looked at her consideringly. 'I take it that you still won't give up your waitressing work?'

She shook her head. 'You know I can't do that, Nikolai.'

Their conflicting needs hovered in the air between them but Nikolai knew that it would be dishonest to make her any promises. Not unless he was sure he could keep them...

'In that case, you have to be prepared for me to travel—because that's what much of my work entails. If you're free to come with me, so much the better—but if not, then I will need to go on my own. Oh, and maybe we should venture out a little beyond the bedroom from now on. And if you're going to start regularly accompanying me to social events, then you really will have to let the stubborn pride thing go.'

She creased her face up in a frown. 'What do you mean?'

'You're going to have to start letting me provide you with a suitable wardrobe. You can't keep borrowing dresses from Emma at the last minute.' He slipped his hand between her legs and saw her eyes darken. 'Can you?'

Zara swallowed as she tried to quell the rising tide of desire—but she was lost. She was about to bury her principles and take whatever it was that Nikolai wanted to offer her, because she loved him too much to walk away. And because there was a small spark of hope deep inside her, which made her wonder if he could ever open his cold and empty heart and find some warmth within.

He would give her a key to his house, and the price for that would be that she would allow him to clothe her as he saw fit. And she would let him because she loved him and would never give up hoping that one day he might love her back.

Love had weakened her and desire had sapped what strength was left, allowing her to morph into being a wealthy man's commodity; his mistress.

CHAPTER THIRTEEN

'SO YOU'LL be back…when?'

With a smile, Nikolai removed Zara's arms from around his neck and reluctantly pulled her dress back down in place. He had planned to say goodbye to her, yes—a lingering kiss at the door of his Kensington house, perhaps. What he had not planned had been that rather frantic kiss which had quickly escalated into an urgent and very erotic coupling up against the wall of the bedroom. But that was what she did to him. Still did to him. Intoxicated him so that he couldn't think straight.

'I'll be back at the weekend,' he murmured. 'Jet-lagged and probably very bad-tempered, but at least while I'm in New York I should get the chance of an uninterrupted night's sleep—without you tempting me every minute of every day.'

'I don't do anything to tempt you, Nikolai.'

'Oh, yes, you do. You exist.' He gave a low laugh. 'And don't be so coy, *milaya moya*. You know damned well the effect you have on me.' He looked at her for a long moment. 'I wish you were coming with me,' he said suddenly.

Zara felt the little leap of her heart but she shook her head with a smile. Because hadn't she decided that she *needed* these breaks from him, when he went away on business? Needed them to assure herself that she *could* function without him and that it was good to practise doing exactly that. To get used to living without him in case it ended tomorrow.

'Well, I can't,' she said. 'I'm a working girl.'

His mouth hardened, because the independent streak he had once so admired had become nothing but a millstone around their necks. Her insistence on working for little more than a pittance kept her away from his side—and weren't mistresses supposed to be always available?

'So you are,' he agreed drily. 'In which case you'd better go and put your panties back on and I'll see you at the weekend. Do we have anything in the diary?'

'A party in Primrose Hill the evening you get back.'

He pulled a face. 'Damn.'

'We don't have to go.'

'No, we don't.' He planted a last kiss on her lips. 'But I think we ought to. Someone from the government who's in charge of promoting green energy in south-east Asia is going to be there and I'd like to talk to him.'

'Okay.' Zara stood at the door, watching as he got into the back of the limousine, realising how many different balls he juggled to keep his empire going. He flashed her a brief smile but she could see that already his thoughts were elsewhere and that he was reaching in his briefcase for paperwork to do on the way to the airport. He worked hard, she'd realised very early on. In fact, he did everything hard. Played, partied, made love, made millions.

She shut the front door, realising that all her own unanswered questions about what she was going to do with her life had become largely academic. Because she knew now that she'd boxed herself into a corner the moment she had agreed to start living with Nikolai. Her future was as uncertain as it had ever been—maybe even more so. There was now no possibility of going away to agricultural college to restart her course—because then she would see hardly anything of him. And he wouldn't put up with that, she recognised. He just about tolerated her waitressing work—as long as it didn't eat into their evenings together.

These days they went out as a couple much more than they'd ever done before, with Zara sporting one of the many exclusive items he insisted on buying for her and which now hung in the closet. She still liked to use Emma's designs wherever possible, but there were a whole host of other things which it seemed were essential to her wardrobe and which her friend couldn't possibly supply. Soft, leather boots and spiky, sexy shoes. Fragile little wisps of lacy underwear. There were day-dresses and sharp little skirts with silk blouses—as well as satin nightgowns which were never designed to be worn for very long.

She would have been a liar if she'd denied enjoying the clothes and finally she could understand why they were essential to her new life. She'd quickly realised that people were intensely interested in her Russian oligarch and that, in a way, what she wore reflected on him. She didn't particularly like the attention his presence always attracted, but she was learning to deal with it.

And if sometimes she stopped to think about how little had changed, well—she quickly pushed those thoughts away. What was the point of dwelling on the fact that his feelings for her hadn't deepened? She couldn't really start complaining about it, could she? Not when he'd warned her at the very beginning what kind of man he was. It was *her* who foolishly kept that little spark of hope alight. Who prayed that one day he might open his heart to her.

She'd packed in loads of jobs to coincide with his trip to New York and the busy days gave her life some kind of structure. Made her feel she had some purpose instead of just idling around, waiting for the return of her lover. And it meant that she had her own—modest—source of income, independent of him. She'd already decided to buy him something from her modest salary—a little welcome home gift—something she could give to *him*, to show him how much she'd missed him. Show him how much she cared, in a way she never dared express with words.

The day before he was due home, Zara went to work at a directors' lunch, right in the very heart of the City. It was a long and boozy affair and one of the executives she knew well by sight fixed her with a curious look as she began to hand out the coffee.

'Is it true that you know Nikolai Komarov?' he questioned.

The cup she was holding rattled as she saw several whoozy heads turn quickly in her direction. 'Er, yes. Yes, I do.'

'Good God! How come?'

Stupidly, Zara could feel a flush beginning to stain her neck. What could she say—that he'd picked her up at a party she'd been gatecrashing and it had taken off from there in an explosion of sexual chemistry which had since shown no sign of abating? *You're not being paid to satisfy this man's curiosity,* she told herself. *He's a client, not a friend.* 'Oh, it's a long story. Er, will you excuse me?' she added hurriedly as she scooped up an empty coffee pot from the table. 'I'd better go and refill this.'

She managed to finish the job without further interrogation and later on she met Emma for a drink, expecting her friend to be bursting with excitement about the
fact that the chief buyer at Nikolai's New York store had
requested a meeting, with a view to commissioning a
future collection from her.

But Emma was not bursting with excitement. In fact,
she looked uncharacteristically glum as they sat down
at a corner table with two glasses of wine and a packet
of salted peanuts.

'Don't tell me they've cancelled the meeting?' asked
Zara anxiously.

'No, no—that's all still going ahead.'

'So why the long face?'

There was a pause as Emma licked some salt from
her finger and when she looked up her expression was
uncomfortable. 'Um, is everything...*okay* between you
and Nikolai?'

Zara frowned. 'What kind of a question is that?'

There was another pause. 'This is very difficult for
me, Zara. Especially because I really like Nikolai and
he's opened up a load of doors for me.'

'Emma, stop it—you're scaring me. What is it?'

'This.' Pulling a newspaper from her bag, Emma
threw it down on the table. 'I know you don't read the
tabloids and it's probably all a pack of lies, but...'

Zara snatched the paper up. It was folded so that the
society pages were open—with its usual batch of PR
plants thinly disguised as articles. And at the top of the
page was a picture of Nikolai, taken near some stunning
looking house, with a woman beside him who was even
more stunning.

Zara hadn't seen the latest blockbuster adventure
film which was currently smashing records at the box
office but she knew that the French actress pictured with

Nikolai was starring as the obligatory love interest. And one look at her gamine beauty told her exactly why.

Her throat dried and her heart pounded as her eyes scanned the text. It said that they'd attended a party together. It said that they'd been engrossed in each other's company. It said that he'd given her a lift home.

Of course he had.

It also said that the actress was currently promoting her new film in…

Zara's mouth dried as the two words leapt off the page and punched her in the eyes.

New York!

She put the newspaper back down, noticing that her hands were trembling. 'Thanks for showing me,' she said hoarsely and drank down a large mouthful of wine. 'Can I keep this?'

'Zara—'

'No. Don't say anything. It's *fine*, Emma—honestly. I'm not under any illusions about my affair with Nikolai. I mean, do you really think I thought it was going to last?'

She managed to sustain the brave face until she was back home—or, rather, back at Nikolai's house—and then she went outside into the beautiful gardens as she thought about what she was going to do.

She remembered the night she had come here, oblivious to the fact that Nikolai had secretly summoned her to work for him, and she had seen him standing at the other end of the lawn, his eyes gleaming with ice-fire as he'd watched her. He had wanted her for all kinds of reasons and she had wanted him. It had been that simple. Her desire for him seemed to have been woven into her DNA and nothing which had happened since had made that desire lessen.

But what of the future? The future she had resolutely tried not to think about since they'd been reunited? Had she really been stupid enough to nurture hope that they might have a future *together* when international actresses of great natural beauty were there for the taking?

She'd just assumed...

What? That he was giving her fidelity? Why would she think that when he had never offered her his fidelity? Never offered her anything more than the physical attraction between them which burned so fiercely. Not even when they'd got back together after their break. The brief episodes of closeness they'd shared hadn't really deepened, had they? And she had just turned a blind eye to it, caring more about smoothing over the surface of their life together than having the courage to explore what lay beneath it. What a pathetic person she was. Why wouldn't a man treat you with contempt when you had shown him that you were prepared to settle for so little?

The homecoming she had planned for him was abandoned—the arty book of photographs of Moscow she'd bought was banished to the back of the wardrobe by hands splashed with her own hot tears. She'd planned on wearing some very naughty underwear—or at least some of it. She'd planned a saucy seduction when they got back from their party—but now all those plans made her feel sick.

Why, wasn't she behaving like some kind of high-class hooker—the kind of woman she had always despised?

The hours until his return ticked by with excruciating slowness until eventually he rang to say that he was on his way back from the airport. She paced the floor until she heard the sound of his car drawing up outside and then the slamming of the front door, and Zara mentally composed herself to greet him. She wasn't going to scream or shout or get hysterical. She was going to be grown-up and as calm as she could.

She had given the housekeeper the afternoon off— much to the woman's surprise—and she supposed it *was* ironic that she should start behaving like the mistress of the house just before she left it. Her heart hammering, Zara went to wait for him in the big sun-room at the back of the house where the French windows were opened to the fragrant scent of the summer evening. On one of the coffee tables lay the newspaper, folded to show the black and white photo of her beautiful, duplicitous lover.

'Zara?'

'I'm in here!'

Her heart twisted with pain as she heard the sound of his footsteps approaching—a sound so unique and distinctive to him. How on earth could she have learned to know and love that particular sound in so short a time?

Nikolai halted in the doorway, his eyes narrowing at the sight of her frozen stance as she turned her unsmiling face to his. The last time he'd been away she had greeted his homecoming with all the pent up passion of a woman who had been left by a man while he went away to fight a war. She had hurled herself into his arms and covered his face with a thousand kisses and started tugging hungrily at his tie. But not tonight. Tonight her face was pale and there were shadows beneath her eyes. And there was no soft silk-satin caressing the curves of her body, either. Instead she wore a pair of jeans and a T-shirt which bore the defiant and faded logo of her old college. Weren't they supposed to be going straight out to a party?

'Hello, Zara,' he said softly.

'Hello, Nikolai.'

He raised his eyebrows. 'No kiss?'

Did she kiss him and pretend nothing had happened? Maybe ask him later, when his guard was down and he might blurt out the truth, however hurtful that might be.

How sad was *that*?

She still hadn't got it, had she? If he was seeing other women then there *was* no getting round him and neither should there be. The relationship was essentially over—it just depended on whether she wanted it to have a painful, protracted death or do the kindest thing and kill it off quickly.

'You're not dressed for the party,' he observed, when still she didn't move.

'No.'

'You don't want to go?'

'Not really.' She sucked in a deep breath and looked at him. 'How was New York?'

'Somehow I get the feeling there's a sting in the tail of that question.'

'And is it guilt which gives you that feeling, Nikolai?'

'*Guilt?*' His mouth tightened with growing comprehension as he pulled off his jacket and threw it onto one of the sofas. Impatiently, he loosened his tie—as if it had been a noose hanging around his neck. 'If I am to be accused of something, isn't it only fair to let the prisoner know what he is being accused of?'

Prisoner? His bizarre choice of description jarred. Zara shook her head, searching for words which would allow her to keep her dignity—and not make her sound like some discordant fishwife. And acknowledging that there was no point in berating him just because—for all his money and possessions—he could not give her the one thing she most wanted.

'How was Marie-Claire?'

'Who?'

She swallowed. Was he going to make a fool of her into the bargain? Effecting ignorance and making her wonder if she was going crazy? 'The French actress you're so close to!'

'The French actress I'm so close to,' he repeated slowly.

'In every sense!'

'I don't know what you're talking about.'

'This is what I'm talking about!' She picked up the newspaper and shoved it at him. 'Here it is, in black and white! Deny it now, if you dare!'

Nikolai looked down at the photo and gave a ghostly smile of recognition. There had been many photos like this published over the years. Sometimes the images had been faithful to the truth and sometimes they had been as far away from it as it was possible to imagine. A captured split second when someone smiled at you and it looked as if you were in your own private little world of love. He had learned many things during his time in the public eye and one of those had been that the camera could be a very unreliable witness.

'You'd believe this *rag*?' he said contemptuously. 'Without bothering to ask me first?'

'Who is she?' Zara demanded.

'I thought you knew exactly who she was! Why should I bother answering your accusations since you already seem to have made your mind up?'

'She's just been in New York!'

'Along with about ten million others!'

Her heart was racing and her mouth felt like sandpaper. 'Don't you think you owe me the courtesy of an explanation, Nikolai?' she questioned quietly.

'And don't you owe *me* the courtesy of showing me a little trust?'

Zara blinked at him. *He* was in the wrong, surely—and now he was twisting it round and making *her* feel as if she'd done something wrong. 'When was the picture taken?'

With a weary sigh, he walked over to the cabinet where the drinks were kept and poured himself a small glass of vodka. He drank only a little of it before putting the glass down and turning to stare at her. 'It was taken while we were on a break—'

'See!'

'I went to a party and she was there. We talked and she asked me for a lift home.'

'Which you, of course, gave her?'

'It seemed ungentlemanly to refuse.'

'And we all know how much of a gentleman you can be in the back of cars, Nikolai!'

He raised his eyebrows. 'Why don't you just come right out and ask me if I slept with her, Zara?'

'Did you?'

'No, I damned well didn't!' he exploded, smashing his fist down on the cupboard so that the glass wobbled and splashed vodka down the side. 'I haven't slept with anyone since I first laid eyes on you. I haven't wanted to. In fact, since the moment I met you—it's like other women don't even exist! I can't seem to get enough of you.'

She bit her lip—because didn't he make that sound more like some sort of fierce sexual obsession than anything really meaningful? 'I find that very hard to believe.'

'Oh, I'll bet you do,' he snapped. 'What does it take to convince you, Zara? I thought I'd take things slowly.

Show you how much I care for you in *real* ways. So I
didn't object when you insisted on continuing with your
waitressing—even though the money they pay you is
ludicrous. I admired your independence, if you must
know. And I like those little presents you buy me when
I go away.'

'Nikolai—'.

'No.' He shook his head. 'You go on and on about
wanting to be my equal—but emotionally you don't have
the courage to try. You dared to be tender with me the
first time we made out—but now it's as if you're holding
back all the time. You used to make me dig deep inside
myself. I'd never have found out about my mother if it
hadn't been for your damned persistence. Sometimes I
resented it, but at least you made me confront things.
You made me feel *alive*. But not any more. Now all I
get from you is precisely—' he snapped his fingers and
his face tightened '—nothing.'

Her fingers flew to her lips in distress. 'Nikolai—'

'I've given you more than I've ever given any woman
and I don't know whether there's anything left to give—
because I get nothing back. Nothing! You affect not to
care about my money or power and yet, deep down, I
think that you despise them. They're all you see—instead
of the man underneath—the man who stupidly thought
you might be able to look beneath all the trappings.' He
bent to pick up his jacket and headed for the door and it
wasn't until Zara heard him talking on his phone to his
driver that she realised he was actually *going out*!

'Where are you going?' she yelled.

'To the party! If I get such an empty reception at
home, then maybe I'll try to find a little comfort elsewhere. And let's face it—' she could hear the grim note

in his voice '—if I'm going to be accused of something I might as well get the benefits of it!'

She heard the door slam just as she began to frame his name and she dashed through the hall to open it just in time to see his car pulling away. For a moment she contemplated sprinting up the road after it, but the powerful car was already down by the electronic gates, its tail lights flashing. Her heart slamming, she stared at the gates closed behind it. *He'd gone to the party!* He'd spoken to her more honestly than he'd ever done before and then he had walked out.

And suddenly she saw her own part in what had gone wrong.

She had accused him of infidelity—she had wanted to believe the very worst of him—was it any wonder that their relationship hadn't deepened when she had been sitting on the sidelines just waiting for him to step out of line? Yet he had never given her any reason to believe that he was interested in other women, had he? She wondered if her lack of trust was driven by his reluctance to offer her any long-term future—or just her general insecurity that a man like Nikolai should be living with someone like her.

So had they now reached a stalemate—with each of them too scared to proceed any further? She because she was afraid of getting hurt and Nikolai because he simply didn't know how to express emotion?

Distractedly, Zara stared out at the beautiful garden. Yet would a man who could have any woman he wanted bother living with someone unless he felt *something*?

And meanwhile he had walked out on her. Gone to some fancy party deciding that he was newly single and where any woman with a pulse would start coming onto him.

'No!' The strangled word was torn from her throat as

she grabbed the invitation from the mantelpiece. Because what was the point of nurturing hope if you didn't let it spark into an almighty flame big enough to melt doubt and uncertainty? What was the point of playing safe if that caused suspicion and unhappiness? Wasn't it time to tell Nikolai exactly how much she loved him—to let it out into the open and see what happened?

She ran outside and then, minutes later, she was out on the main street outside the gates, searching for a cab. She saw one on the other side of the road and, to a cacophony of angry horns, she dodged the traffic to hail it down and jump in the back.

'Take me to Primrose Hill,' she said breathlessly as the driver turned off the yellow light. 'As quickly as possible.'

The party was being held in a house which was as imposing as she had imagined and as she saw the immaculately dressed people going inside she suddenly realised how frightful she must look with her flushed cheeks and messy hair. But she didn't care. There was something much more important at stake here than her appearance. She just prayed that she hadn't left it too late...

She rang the doorbell and the uniformed butler raised his eyebrows.

'Yes?' he questioned unhelpfully.

'I'm here for the party!'

His face twisted into an I-don't-believe-you expression. 'And do you have an invitation, madam?'

'Yes. Here it is.' Thank heavens she'd had the foresight to bring it with her. She thrust the card at him and pushed past him, not caring what he thought.

The murmur of voices and chink of glasses directed her footsteps up to the first-floor drawing room and when

Zara walked in there was a pin-drop silence. But then, maybe that was because she was the only person in the room who was wearing faded jeans and a T-shirt bearing the legend 'Agricultural Students Do It In Fields'.

All eyes seemed to be fixed on her but she was aware of only one pair. She could see Nikolai on the far side of the room and she couldn't make out whether he looked shocked, furious, amused—or all three. But suddenly she didn't care. She had to tell him. Even if it *was* too late—he had to know how she felt.

She walked right up to him and the blonde woman who had been smiling up at him now looked at him askance, as if an axe-murderer had just muscled in on their conversation.

'Nikolai?' she ventured, in a tiny little voice which matched her tiny couture-clad frame.

But Nikolai didn't appear to have even heard the woman. His narrowed eyes were fixed and intent. 'Zara.'

'Yes,' she breathed as the enormity of what she was about to do hit her.

'This is a surprise.'

His wry understatement made her draw a deep breath. She supposed she could ask him to accompany her to another room, where they might have some peace and privacy. But Zara was afraid that if she waited a second longer then her nerve would leave her and she would never dare say the words which now bubbled out of her.

'I love you, Nikolai Komarov,' she said, in a quiet urgent voice. 'I've loved you for so long that I've forgotten what it's like not to love you—only I was too scared to show it before.'

He didn't say a word, just continued to stare at her with a steady blue gaze which was as cold as ice.

Zara drew in another deep breath. 'I was scared that if I started to show you what I felt—that it would open up the floodgates to something so powerful that it would sweep me away on its tide. And I thought you didn't want love like that.'

For a moment there was a silence so long that it felt as if time had stretched itself out, like a piece of elastic. *Say something*, she urged silently. *Say anything, but at least say* something.

But there was no smile and no words. Nikolai just stood there as silent and as unmoving as a block of stone and Zara could see the look of shock and something else which had darkened his eyes. Something which looked a little like fear—from a man who didn't do fear. But he didn't do love either, did he? He'd told her that in no uncertain terms.

As Zara listened to the heavy silence she realised that her worst nightmare had come true. The gamble hadn't paid off. He *didn't* love her. Didn't even care enough to murmur a few placatory words, which might have allowed her to save face. He was standing looking at her as if she were some kind of madwoman—while the rest of the room looked on with a mixture of amused horror.

'I'm so sorry,' she whispered. 'I should never have come here.'

Unsteadily, she turned and stumbled from the room and the silence began to grow into an astonished roar as she made her way downstairs, brushing past the sanctimonious face of the butler and out onto the street.

Shuddering, she gripped onto the iron railing outside the house as she sucked in several deep breaths, but she still felt weak and dizzy—as if she was about to faint.

But she couldn't afford to do that—not with people still arriving. *I have to get away*, she told herself fiercely. *I have to move away from here before I make an even bigger fool of myself.*

Blindly, she made her way to the end of the street, her eyes blurred with tears, the acid taste of dryness at the back of her throat as she tried to swallow down the sobs which were building in intensity. The glimpse of green at the end of the street made her make her way towards it, some instinct propelling her towards the light and space of Primrose Hill. And that was when she heard running footsteps behind her and the sound of someone calling her name.

She would have recognised his footsteps and the sexy lilt of Nikolai's Russian accent from miles away but Zara didn't let her own step falter because the last thing she wanted was to face him. What was she supposed to do, turn around and tell him she was fine and that she didn't care that she'd humiliated herself by telling him she loved him in front of a room full of snooty people?

'Zara!'

Ignoring him, she tore into the park and then began to run up the hill, past the iconic lamp-posts. It had always been a favourite place of hers for picnics—a long ride on the Northern Line ending in a cute little hill which made you feel you were flying.

But not today. Today her feet felt leaden and she prayed that Nikolai might have taken the hint and gone back to his party. *Leave me in peace to nurse my wounds,* she prayed silently. *Don't make it any worse than it already is. Don't let me keep reliving the moment when I confessed my love for you in a room full of people and you stared at me as if I had just offered you a goblet of pure poison.*

'Zara!'

The voice was closer now. Almost upon her, in fact. And then she could feel his hand on her arm and it was holding her and not letting her go. In fact, he was turning her round as if it were a practised dance move and his face was tense, his eyes dark with some unknown emotion. Furiously, she began to pummel her fists against his chest.

'*Let me go!*'

'No!'

'Let me go or I'll scream my head off!'

'I'll let you go when you've heard me out, Zara. Please.'

It was a word he used so rarely that for a moment she hesitated. 'Why are you here? To laugh at me?'

'Zara. Zara. My sweet Zara—'

'No!' she interrupted furiously. 'I don't want to hear your lying words!'

'But I've never lied to you, Zara. You know that.'

A sob erupted from the back of her throat as he pulled her closer. 'Just leave me be, Nikolai,' she whispered brokenly. 'Don't make it worse than it already is.'

'I'm going to make it better.'

'You can't. You can't make it better.'

He took hold of both her shoulders then—so that she couldn't look anywhere except at his face. 'Not even if I tell you that I love you?' he demanded quietly. 'Or that I've been a fool? That I was dumbfounded when you walked into that room—your beautiful face alight with love and excitement? And that I didn't realise how much courage it must have taken for you to come right out and tell me how you felt.'

'Nikolai—'

'No.' Shaking his head, he moved his face a little

closer, so that their eyes were on a collision course—hers tear-filled and wary and the brightest green he could ever remember seeing. 'Hear me out. Let me say what I should have said back there. That I didn't realise the value of what I had until I almost lost it.' Might still lose it, he realised bitterly as he saw the tremble of her lips. Because mightn't Zara—his sweet and sexy Zara—have decided that she could no longer tolerate a man who was made of such emotional ice? Could he honestly blame her if that was the way she felt and found herself unable to forgive him—especially as he had failed so spectacularly to even acknowledge her outpouring of love?

'It was a shock,' he said simply, in as honest an admission of his true feelings as he had ever given. 'To have you declare your love in front of all those people. After a lifetime of keeping my private life private and of hiding the way I felt, it was—as you once said to me—a bit of a bombshell. But my reaction was something which was bone-deep—the lessons I learned in childhood don't just suddenly disappear—even if you want them to. Early on, I discovered pretty quickly that it was necessary to block out high emotion. Not to react when a longed-for letter failed to appear. Nor to show fear when you were left alone for days without a word.'

'Nikolai—'

'No,' he said again. 'I have to tell you this. After you'd gone, people began to cluster round me—with looks of sympathy on their faces, as if something terrible had just happened. And that's when I realised that something terrible *would* happen, if I didn't find you and admit what's been building in my heart and in my mind for so long. Only I had to come close to losing it before I could find the courage to express it.'

He sucked in a deep breath, wanting to do his love

justice. To honour the woman who stood before him, after all she had done for him. All she had given him.

Yet when he fished around his extensive vocabulary he found that the most simple words were the most profound. Maybe that was why they could be the most difficult of all to say.

'I love you,' he said and then sucked in an unsteady breath. 'I was lost and lonely as a little boy and I never really learnt how to love because nobody had ever shown me how. And no one did…until I met you.'

She stared at him and she knew that everything he said was true. He *had* never lied to her and neither would he squander words he had once thought himself incapable of saying. Mutely, she swallowed down the great lump in her throat.

'I love you so very much, Zara Evans,' he whispered. 'A whole lifetime wouldn't be enough to tell you just how much, and that's why I was wondering—' he lifted her fingertips to his lips and his blue eyes blazed ice-fire at her as he kissed each one in turn '—if you would do me the honour of becoming my wife?'

The emotion of the moment was so great—the shock of his declaration so moving—that words were still stubbornly refusing to come. Again Zara nodded her head, blinking back tears and realising that this great burning feeling in her chest was her heart on fire with love for her darling Nikolai.

But Nikolai didn't need words. Tenderly, he gathered her close and bent his mouth to hers—and her kiss gave him the only answer he really wanted.

EPILOGUE

NIKOLAI and Zara were married in the Russian church in London—with Zara repeating some of her vows in the language she had vowed to learn, even though her new husband warned her that the Cyrillic alphabet wasn't easy.

'Ah, but I like a challenge,' she'd answered, raising her lips to be kissed.

'Do you?' he murmured back.

'I agreed to marry you, didn't I?'

He laughed. 'You certainly did.'

For the ceremony, she wore a simple, silk-satin dress designed by Emma, who had finally managed to persuade her mother that the Gourmet International staff needed a brand new uniform. Consequently, the waitresses now looked chic as well as professional and bookings had soared—though, as Emma's mother sighed, she seemed to have lost some of her best girls to their millionaire clients because of it!

But none of her friends were working on the day the newly-weds took over the famous mirrored ballroom of the Granchester Hotel for their wedding reception. Zara had been too dazed with love to really care about table plans and favours, or whether she wanted chocolate wedding cake, or a traditional fruit version. Her only specification had been that the flowers should be country blooms—as if they'd just been picked from a cottage garden. Which was why the vast room was scented with masses of blowsy roses, which were far more fragrant than the hothouse variety.

Security was tight because the best man happened to be a US Senator—and Sergei arrived with a new—and younger—blonde on his arm. The day went without a glitch and hearing the excited chatter of the guests was strangely gratifying. It was, Zara realised, the first real party they had thrown.

But for the new Mrs Komarov, the best bit of all was when Nikolai stood up to make his speech—looking unbelievably gorgeous in his morning suit with his dark gold hair gleaming beneath the spangled light of the chandeliers.

He thanked Emma for designing the dress and for being such a wonderful bridesmaid and he made a few jokes about the differences between Russian men and English men. But then his face grew solemn as he turned to Zara, and, although everyone in the room could hear what he said, he seemed to be speaking just to her.

'I've been trying to work out words which would do my new wife justice,' he said slowly. 'But it's proved a tough call. There's no need for me to tell you that she's beautiful—because you can all see that for yourselves. I could tell you that she's hard-working and strong and independent—but those of you who know her will already realise that. I could tell you that she makes me laugh more than anyone I've ever met. That she lights up a room when she walks into it and every minute spent away from her leaves a little ache in my heart. I could tell you that she has taught me so much about life that is important. But most of all…' at this he smiled into her eyes and raised his glass of champagne '…she has taught me the meaning of love. And I love her,' he said simply. 'I love her so very much. So I ask you please to raise your glasses to my wonderful wife and to drink to Zara.'

'To Zara!' the room echoed and then burst into rapturous applause.

But Zara was too busy scrabbling inside her white satin handbag to fish out a crumpled-up tissue. Had Nikolai—the notoriously private Nikolai—just stood up in front of a roomful of people and told them how much he loved her?

Nikolai laughed softly as he took the tissue from her trembling fingers and began to dab at her cheeks. 'Better now?' he murmured.

She sniffed. 'Much better.'

'Should I ask why you're crying?'

'Because I'm so happy.'

'I thought so.'

She thought his own eyes looked suspiciously bright as he pulled her close against him. But that was okay. Everyone knew that people always cried at weddings.

MILLS & BOON®

are proud to present our...

Book of the Month

Come to Me
by Linda Winstead Jones

from Mills & Boon® Intrigue

Lizzie needs PI Sam's help in looking for her lost
half-sister. Sam's always had a crush on Lizzie.
But moving in on his former partner's daughter
would be *oh-so-wrong*...

Available 15th April

*Something to say about our Book of the Month?
Tell us what you think!*

millsandboon.co.uk/community
facebook.com/romancehq
twitter.com/millsandboonuk

MODERN™

PASSION AND THE PRINCE
by Penny Jordan

Prince Marco di Lucchesi can't hide his haughty disdain for Lily Wrightington—or his violent attraction to her! Can he trust himself to offer the protection she seeks *without* unleashing his passion?

ALESSANDRO'S PRIZE
by Helen Bianchin

Determined to get on with her newly single life, a break in Milan sounds ideal to Lily Parisi. Until she bumps into Alessandro del Marco, an enigmatic face from her past, and her plans come completely undone…

WIFE IN THE SHADOWS
by Sara Craven

In society's spotlight, Count Angelo Manzini bestows dutiful kisses on his apparently biddable new bride, Elena. But behind closed doors, Angelo is captivated by his countess's defiance…

AN INCONVENIENT OBSESSION
by Natasha Tate

Ethan Hardesty has it all…apart from Cate Carrington—the girl he loved and lost. But now the Carrington family's island is up for auction, providing him with the perfect opportunity to take her into the bargain!

On sale from 20th May 2011
Don't miss out!

*Available at WHSmith, Tesco, ASDA, Eason
and all good bookshops*
www.millsandboon.co.uk

MODERN

FOR DUTY'S SAKE
by Lucy Monroe

Angele refuses to become Crown Prince Zahir's unloved wife out of duty; she will let him go free...but on one condition. The proud Sheikh must give her the wedding night she has dreamed of!

MR AND MISCHIEF
by Kate Hewitt

Sardonic Jason Kingsley is used to women falling at his feet, but relationships are not for him. So why does he find Emily Wood, with her misguided belief in the power of love, irresistibly attractive?

THE BROODING STRANGER
by Maggie Cox

Seeking refuge from her past, Karen Ford comes to Ireland with no intention of getting involved with any man. *Especially* not the brooding stranger she meets one fateful day, who makes a shockingly intimate proposition...

THE GIRL HE NEVER NOTICED
by Lindsay Armstrong

Tycoon Cam Hillier requires a date for this season's fundraising party, and turns to his PA, Liz Montrose, in desperation! Cam's never noticed Liz before...but with no sensible suits or glasses for her to hide behind, that's about to change!

On sale from 3rd June 2011
Don't miss out!

The Privileged and the Damned
by Kimberly Lang

Lily needs a fresh start—and, fingers crossed, she's found one. After all, why would any of the hot-shot Marshall dynasty even *think* to look beyond her humble façade? Until she catches the roving eye of infamous heartbreaker Ethan Marshall...

The Big Bad Boss
by Susan Stephens

Heath Stamp, the ultimate bad-boy-done-good, is now rich, arrogant and ready to raze his family estate to the ground. If Bronte tries to stop him he'll happily take her down with him. For Heath Stamp has gone from bad...to irresistible!

Ordinary Girl in a Tiara
by Jessica Hart

Caro Cartwright's had enough of romance—she's after a quiet life. Until an old school friend begs her to stage a gossip-worthy royal diversion! Reluctantly, Caro prepares to masquerade as a European prince's latest squeeze...

Tempted by Trouble
by Liz Fielding

Upon meeting smooth-talking Sean McElroy, Elle's 'playboy' radar flashes red, and she tries to ignore the traitorous flicker of attraction! Yet are these two misfits the perfect match?

On sale from 3rd June 2011
Don't miss out!

Available at WHSmith, Tesco, ASDA, Eason and all good bookshops

www.millsandboon.co.uk

2 FREE BOOKS
AND A SURPRISE GIFT

We would like to take this opportunity to thank you for reading this Mills & Boon® book by offering you the chance to take TWO more specially selected books from the Modern™ series absolutely FREE! We're also making this offer to introduce you to the benefits of the Mills & Boon® Book Club™—

- **FREE home delivery**
- **FREE gifts and competitions**
- **FREE monthly Newsletter**
- **Exclusive Mills & Boon Book Club offers**
- **Books available before they're in the shops**

Accepting these FREE books and gift places you under no obligation to buy, you may cancel at any time, even after receiving your free books. Simply complete your details below and return the entire page to the address below. You don't even need a stamp!

YES Please send me 2 free Modern books and a surprise gift. I understand that unless you hear from me, I will receive 4 superb new books every month for just £3.30 each, postage and packing free. I am under no obligation to purchase any books and may cancel my subscription at any time. The free books and gift will be mine to keep in any case.

Ms/Mrs/Miss/Mr _____ Initials _____

_____

Surname _____

Address _____

_____

_____ Postcode _____

E-mail _____

Send this whole page to: Mills & Boon Book Club, Free Book Offer, FREEPOST NAT 10298, Richmond, TW9 1BR

Offer valid in UK only and is not available to current Mills & Boon Book Club subscribers to this series. Overseas and Eire please write for details. We reserve the right to refuse an application and applicants must be aged 18 years or over. Only one application per household. Terms and prices subject to change without ~~~~ Offer expires 31st July 2011. As a result of this application, you may receive offers from Harlequin ~~~ carefully selected companies. If you would prefer not to share in this opportunity please ~~~~ Manager, PO Box 676, Richmond, TW9 1WU.

~~~~stered trademark owned by Harlequin (UK) Limited.
~~~ as a trademark. The Mills & Boon® Book Club™ is being used as a trademark.